WINELL ROAD

BOOK ONE

KATE FOSTER

Winell Road by Kate Foster
Second Edition

First Edition published 2015

Text Copyright © Kate Foster
Cover Illustration Copyright © Paul Mudie
Cover Design by E.L. Wicker
All Rights Reserved.

ISBN-10: 0-9953629-1-2
ISBN-13: 978-0-9953629-1-8

To the worker of Tonbridge.

Forever.

CHAPTER ONE

THE ENCOUNTER

The roaring crowd leaped to their feet, and Jack performed a triumphant skid across the concrete. "Goal!" he cried, springing up and patting his invisible teammates on the back. Pulling away from the imagined embrace, Jack sighed. He hated summer break; it was always so boring. Plus, the Woodlands under-13 squad took time out from training and matches too, so the only soccer he could play was against himself. Still, only two weeks and he'd be back on the pitch, in the company of *normal* people.

He bent down and picked up his soccer ball. Five more minutes and he'd head inside. Maybe Dad would've finished work; maybe they'd be able to watch a movie together. He still had to catch up on the final *Indiana Jones* he'd borrowed from Andy forever ago. Chances were Dad would still be down in the basement. Still, Jack could dream.

But as he straightened darkness crept over him, over the ground around him. He frowned.

Then he felt it.

Something behind him. Close. Too close.

Jack glanced over his shoulder, his eyes slowly widening. The ball slipped from under his arm and rolled away.

A few feet above him floated a vast, silver sphere with intricate markings and a grooved spiral that finished at a black, central disc. Four enormous legs were spread evenly, and bright lights shone from the base of each one. The strange object was deafeningly silent—no wonder he hadn't heard it lowering down.

Now it hovered, frozen in mid-air. Just... Just looking at him.

Jack stared, his jaw unable to drop any further. He didn't blink. Or move. He couldn't. He didn't even know if he was breathing.

He should run away, anywhere. But it was like his shoes were super-glued to the ground.

The disc began to spin. Slowly at first but soon picking up speed. The wind from it flattened Jack's scruffy brown hair to his scalp like a helmet. His eyes stung from the force.

He lifted up his hands to protect his face and, squinting, he stepped back.

Faster it spun. Dirt kicked up, striking him from every direction. Nearby branches bent in the opposite direction, while flowers lost their battles to remain upright. Jack gasped for air. He crouched to the ground and covered his face. As he peered through his fingers, his ball soared through the air and disappeared into the trees.

He had to run. Whatever was about to happen, he didn't want to find out. This was huge. Massive. Ginormous. Ginormassivous. But another word ran through his mind, over and over.

Abduction.

Just as Jack toppled forward onto his hands and knees, the wind stopped. The branches returned to their original positions, and the flowers, which hadn't snapped, gradually stood back up.

Jack whipped his head up to the sky. Gone; whatever it was, like someone had rubbed it out with a giant eraser. He pirouetted, round and round, his eyes searching wildly. But all he could see were dreary gray clouds joining together, devouring any remaining blue.

Someone else must have seen it!

Jack hunted for anyone else on the street, but there wasn't a flicker of life anywhere. No George pruning his pathetic wilting plants, not even Petula peeping through her curtains. Not a soul. Where had everyone gone?

Mom! She was always in the backyard and definitely would've seen it from there.

Rushing through his front door, Jack hurried through the kitchen and flew out the back door.

Mom wasn't digging at the vegetable patch or weeding in the expansive flowerbeds. There was no movement in the trees backing onto the yard.

The greenhouse!

"Mom!" Jack cried, rushing in through the open door.

"Did you see it?" She wasn't there. He ran back out into the yard, checking the sky again.

"Did you call me, love?"

Jack turned to see his mother step from the greenhouse. "What? But I just looked for you in there," he said, scratching his head.

"Well, there's nowhere else I could've come from. Perhaps I blended in with the sunflowers." She pointed at her outrageously yellow cardigan.

Jack shook off Mom's incredible hiding skills, and dismal joke, and asked again. "Did you see it?"

"See what?"

"The thing in the sky."

"What thing?"

He paused. What should he say? Spaceship? UFO? Flying saucer? Right now, they all sounded ridiculous.

"The thing. The... The big silver thing."

"Umm... I don't think so. What was it? A bird?"

"No... No." Jack blew out a breath through his nose, his shoulders drooping. "It was probably just a helicopter flying low or something." Mom hadn't seen it. That much was clear and, rather than sound like one of the loonies off a Discovery Channel UFO documentary, it was best not to worry her.

"Right. Sorry, love, I was engrossed in my flowers as usual. Have you seen Cedric?"

Cedric the sunflower. "Yeah, looking good, Mom."

Something wet hit Jack's forehead. Then another plop

and a trickle down the back of his white t-shirt.

"Oh no, here comes the rain again. Get yourself in, darling, and I'll come and cook your supper soon," Mom ordered before disappearing into her greenhouse.

As the rain fell heavily, Jack obeyed and retreated indoors. Climbing the stairs to his bedroom, he worried his bottom lip. *Could* he have imagined it? He was pretty expert at daydreaming.

He shook his head. No, there was absolutely no way.

It had been real.

CHAPTER TWO

THE CARD COLLECTION

Another cloudy day. A few drops of rain. A few more. And then the downpour. Jack sighed and stared at the raindrops attacking his window pane.

Two days since *the encounter*, yet now, well, it was like it never happened.

Jack had expected something. Anything. A TV news report, a newspaper article, gossiping neighbors. Even a couple of men in smart black suits, wearing shades and flashing badges; the type who always turn up in sci-fi films when aliens come to Earth. But no, they never showed. But why hadn't they? If the spaceship had been real then it would have shown up on some government radar or satellite thingy. Surely he wasn't the only one on the planet who saw it.

If only he could phone Andy, he'd believe him. As mismatched as they were—Jack, skinny and sporty, Andy Aldred, chubby and studious—they'd been best friends for as long as Jack could remember. There was no one he trusted more. But sadly, as it always was during a school break, Andy was off visiting his mysteriously secret parents and absolutely no contact was allowed.

Full-blown boredom struck.

Sighing again, as loudly as possible this time, Jack tossed his soccer ball into the corner of his bedroom. The same ball that had vanished into the woods on *that* day and miraculously reappeared in his backyard the following morning. Who had returned it? Mom sat at the top of the suspect list. Jack often spotted her pretending to pick flowers and berries in the woods that wrapped around Winell Road like a leafy cloak. Of course, that was just a cover for spying on the neighbors.

The ball bounced from the floor to the wall to the opposite wall and rolled finally to a rest by his feet. He collapsed onto his bed.

There had to be something to do. No matter how much he looked through his telescope, he couldn't magically make the spaceship return.

DS… boring. Books… boring. TV… boring. School tree project… definitely no way!

Jack reached for a pile of cards sitting on his bedside cabinet. He fanned them out in his hands and sat forward, smoothing the creases of his blue checked blanket as he placed them down. He selected a couple to read.

Keu'Plachu

A thin-bodied, tall creature with hyper-sensitive detectors on its head. Originally from Scimerian, it has been spotted on many other planets within the Milky Way. Able to sense movement and sound many kilometers away. A shy being that relies on hearing dangers to flee. It does not engage in physical situations.

Strength:115
Danger:2
Sight:100
Hearing:1800
Intelligence:525

Spodian

A large, winged creature from Iba that camouflages into its surroundings. Extremely intelligent, it can travel at incredible speeds and through all known substances along with whatever touches it.

Strength:201
Danger:50
Sight:2
Hearing:5
Intelligence:1500

Jack loved his alien cards. Well, he used to. He'd been addicted, but since starting sixth grade last year, he'd hardly played with them. The spaceship visit had sparked off a renewed interest, though, and soon after he'd dug his collection out from the bottom of the drawer.

Dad had given him a handful of cards when he was seven and for every birthday since Jack had asked for more. His collection had been approaching fifty when his interest dwindled. He felt bad, considering Dad always went on about how hard they were to find, but collector cards just weren't that cool anymore.

He took the pen and notepad that were bound together with the cards and, flipping to the page containing his most recent list of aliens, crossed out a couple. He added Keu'Plachu and Spodian to the bottom.

"Right, one more," Jack said, counting the names on the page.

Casting his eyes across the display, he noticed the gray edge of a card poking out within the pile.

Weird, all his cards were purple-edged.

He pulled it out and studied it. This one was different. Very different. He read:

Axeinos

BEWARE: True origin unknown. An extremely dangerous, deadly creature wreaking havoc within the Milky Way. It has no true form but takes the shape of other creatures to capture its prey. Can be identified by an occasional flash of its bright red eyes. An expert at mind control.

Strength:175
Danger:1250
Sight:100
Hearing:90
Intelligence:1500

"Awesome!" This was a first—an alien from another galaxy! The first he'd seen anyway.

More than five years he'd been building his collection, how come he'd never seen this card before? Organized wasn't his middle name, so overlooking it was possible. Jack shook his head and studied the card again until noises from outside forced him to look up at his front window. An engine; banging; squeaking doors.

He'd lived at 5 Winell Road all his life, so was pretty tuned in to what was normal. And these sounds didn't come under normal—not for Winell Road at least. *Crash! Bang!* Jack put down his notepad and went to check out what was happening outside.

The street was one seriously boring place to live. With only a handful of houses, of which nearly half were empty, it was just a stupid dead-end road. Or cul-de-sac, as Mom loved to call it. The only way anyone could reach it was up the bumpy, thin track that led off Main Road. Plus, it was mainly occupied by freaks. Nosy Petula Penula, bald, lanky George who had a pee problem, and Mrs. Atkins who Jack hadn't ever seen because she never left her house.

No other kids lived there either. Unless you counted the Fann octuplets, of course. But they were tiny, maybe three or four years old, and followed their mom everywhere.

Jack peered down at the road, and drew in a sharp breath. No way. What was going on? Things just got weirder.

Next door; 4 Winell Road. Empty throughout Jack's entire twelve years of life.

But today, someone was moving in.

CHAPTER THREE

THE NEW NEIGHBORS

"**J**ack! Quick! The new neighbors have arrived. Come and see!"

And Mom confirmed it.

How come he hadn't heard about new neighbors? Mom would've mentioned something before now. She wasn't one to keep things to herself.

Jack made his way down his beanstalk of a house. Sandwiched between Dad's basement workshop and a bizarre dome-shaped attic, which Jack couldn't remember having ever been in, sat four stories. The kitchen on the ground floor, the lounge on the first, then came his bedroom, and his parents' room on top of that. A new take on *Jack and the Beanstalk*.

"Come on, Jack! You'll miss it," Mom squeaked.

Jack rolled his eyes. Amazing how excited she got spying on the neighbors—aka complete weirdos who didn't do anything, ever.

He slumped into the kitchen and found Mom leaning over the sink, staring out the window with her long, graying hair pinned back into a neat bun, and her purple-spotted scarf dipping in the half-filled bowl of soapy water. She didn't even peel her eyes away from the window to acknowledge him.

"Quick, Jack! Come and look," she said, beckoning over her shoulder. "The rain's dried up just in time."

Jack joined her at the sink. Out the window, a white moving-van with the words *CRANK BROS* printed on the side was parked next door. Two stocky men lifted a sofa from the van and carried it clumsily through the front door.

"I think they are the Crank Brothers," Mom said.

Duh! "You think?" Jack said. "How did they get that van up here off Main Road, the track is way too narrow for something that wide."

Mom clearly wasn't listening. "There! That's the daughter." She flapped a pointing finger at the window.

Jack looked.

"She must be *the* tallest girl in the world, look how she has to stoop climbing out the back of the van!" Mom said.

"How old is she?" Jack asked, knowing full well Mom would already have the answer.

"I think about thirteen or so. Oooo, there's her mother."

Jack looked again.

Unsurprisingly, she was as tall as her daughter. In fact, both of them towered above the moving men. It was an odd sight, but Jack hardly expected anything different. Being weird in some way seemed essential for living on Winell Road. The other residents made Mom and Dad look almost normal. Almost.

"Gosh!" bellowed a voice from behind. "What a couple of whoppers!"

Jack jumped back, and Mom let out a squeal. It was Dad, standing in the kitchen doorway.

"Have I missed anything?" He squeezed in the middle, putting an arm around each of their shoulders.

"Not really," Jack said, shifting along.

Mom's hundred-mile-an-hour commentary continued. "The girl's very fashionable, isn't she? I like that outfit of jeans cut off to the knee with the white t-shirt, and the mother is dressed similar to me, look, I'm often in black slacks and a blouse, and I always have a cardigan draped over my shoulders, don't I?" She didn't wait for an answer. "Both mother and daughter have the same striking hair, don't they?"

Jack nodded. This observation was too true. Their hair was eye-catching to say the least—crazy, curly, and bright white.

Apart from their stature and hair, there was something else unusual about them. Jack tilted his head to one side. The mother, in particular... but what? He couldn't put his finger on it.

"Well, that's enough excitement for me," Dad announced, banging his hands on the countertop, making Jack jump again. "I'm headed back to the basement to finish the prototype of the new exercise bike vacuum cleaner. I think it's going to be a winner." And with that he left the room.

Another of Dad's ridiculously useless inventions—inventions Jack was only too used to. The list of things that had not surprisingly failed was endless. The False Nail Soap Dispenser, the Self-Opening Window, and who could forget the Camera Belt. Utter embarrassment.

And many of Jack's birthday presents had been inventions of a sort. The voice-activated bike, which had earned him the name of "The Bike Whisperer" at school, and the Codebreaker, a huge mobile phone Dad said he'd found in the forest and then tampered with. Several absurd additions aside, the phone's main feature was it could break into other people's electronic devices and steal data. Clever—yes. Unethical—absolutely.

A second or two after his departure, Dad returned, poking his balding head around the kitchen door. "Penny, love, don't forget Mrs. Atkins' flowers. You know how upset she gets if she doesn't get them." And, for a second time, he shuffled in his threadbare moccasins out the kitchen.

"Yes, Arthur dear, I'll do them now." Mom sighed. "That's it for me too, then, I suppose. I'd best pick Mrs. Atkins' flowers. She got terribly cross yesterday when I was late. I'll be in the greenhouse, love, let me know if anything exciting happens."

Mom sidestepped out of the room, snatching a final glance out of the window.

Jack rolled his eyes. Such weird people. Anyway, maybe

he'd scope out the new neighbors for a little longer.

Closely examining next door's new female duo, it soon became clear how awkwardly they moved. The young girl was so lanky she didn't seem in control of her limbs, but the mother looked artificial, almost like a robot. Since he'd been ogling out the window, Jack hadn't seen her talk to anyone. In fact, she hadn't even looked at the others. And, at that moment, as the two ladies helped each other lift a wooden chest from the van, her expression was serious and her steps exaggerated. The chest was huge, about the size of an extra-large coffin, and clearly heavy, but she didn't seem to be struggling. Not one bit.

Jack nodded. That must be it. She was freakishly strong. As well as tall. And serious. Like a robot. With unnaturally white hair.

A satisfying conclusion. He could put an end to his snooping; he didn't have the staying power of his mother. Remembering his new collector card upstairs, he left the kitchen ready to engage in some more alien battles.

But as his foot touched the first paisley-patterned stair, he paused. As if a magnet was tempting him back, Jack unwillingly re-entered the kitchen. Not sure what he was expecting to see, or for that matter why he was return-ing at all, he peered in the direction of next door. His eyebrows pinched together, and his heart bounced about furiously.

She stood alone beside the moving van, gawping in the direction of his house.

The mother.

Jack's body stiffened like the dead animals he found in the forest. His unease returned tenfold.

She was standing rigid, staring straight in through his kitchen window, her eyes not appearing to blink or her body to breathe, but her mouth... Yes, her mouth was moving. Her lips making the same shapes, over and over. Repeating the same words again and again.

Jack ducked behind the sink.

Was she looking at him? It couldn't be possible; Mom had hung net curtains up on the window so she could spy on everyone without them knowing. There was no way anyone could see inside, not unless they had their face pressed right up to the glass.

He rose a little and peered over the sink, squinting to help focus on her face.

His insides flipped over.

One of her arms gradually rose, until horizontal. Her index finger extended and pointed right at him, her lips still moving.

Was she pointing at *him*? How did she know he was even there?

Afraid to continue looking but equally afraid to move, Jack remained still, attempting to read her lips. What was she saying? Those words, what were they?

After a few seconds, movement stole his attention as the daughter emerged from the house. As she approached the van, her mother lowered her arm and turned away.

With his heart thudding and his hands quivering, Jack let out the breath he'd been holding as the white-haired duo climbed inside the moving van and out of sight.

Did that really just happen?

Without delay, he sped up to the safety of his bedroom for the second time that week, shutting the door firmly behind him.

CHAPTER FOUR

THE ALMOST FIRST VISIT

J ack slid his hands down his face, pulling at his skin.
He wanted to cry. Or scream. Anything that might
release his frustration. *Why, people, why?*
Mom had just informed him that the new neighbors
were coming over that very afternoon for tea and cakes.
What awful thing had he done to deserve this? For one,
he was still uncomfortable following the staring incident
earlier, and second, tea and cakes meant Mom was baking.
The outcome of which was rarely good.

He lay on his bed trying to muster a grain of energy to
change into—in Mom's exact words—"more suitable at-
tire for the guests." What was wrong with sweats, anyway?

Doing his best not to think about next door's creepy
new owners, Jack wondered what concoctions Mom might
come up with today. He was quite sure she must've tried
every possible combination of ingredients. Ever. But this
was a thought, or rather a hope, he'd had for some time
now, and she still managed to keep them coming.

From the acorn, mixed berry, and brie soufflé, that, for
unknown reasons, didn't puff up as it was supposed to, to

the begonia, parsnip, and strawberry cheesecake, minus the cheese, most of Mom's creations were diabolical.

Occasionally she hit the right notes. Jack had a favorite: the creamy chocolate cherry loaf.

He sighed. It was a last minute invitation, so Mom wouldn't have a great deal of time to put much thought into it. But maybe that was a good thing; he could only wait and see. He crossed his fingers.

Jack dragged his legs to the side of the bed and sat up. He opened and closed a couple of drawers. His closet consisted of mainly joggers, hoodies, and t-shirts. Not a great deal to choose from that Mom wouldn't moan about. So, as he always had to for classier events, he settled on black jeans and a white button-up shirt.

With his pants already in a heap at his feet and now halfway through removing his camouflage tee, Jack's ears homed-in on a noise. He could just make it out over the sound from his TV.

TAP! TAP! TAP!

He froze, both arms caught up in the t-shirt covering his head, and listened. He swiveled in the direction of the muffled tapping and held his breath.

It was coming from the back window. Then, as suddenly as it had begun, it stopped. Jack whipped off his top and examined the area by the window.

Telescope looked normal—perched on its tripod and ready for some stargazing.

His eyes shifted left. Bookcase appeared the same—

books all neat on the shelves.

And then he looked to his right.

The clutter box. Maybe one of his battery-powered gadgets had been left on and was hitting the plastic side. As it was the only reasonable explanation, he went over to search for the culprit.

Dropping to his knees, he rummaged through the tub, checking things that had on/off switches, but the tapping had started again. And it definitely wasn't coming from inside the box.

Jack turned his head to the left. The bookcase.

TAP! TAP! TAP!

On his knees, he shuffled over.

Perhaps an insect had flown in through an open window and somehow got wedged behind a book. It was possible, and probably best to free it now before it found a hiding place and launched a middle-of-the-night attack. Jack shivered.

He surveyed the second shelf, trying to work out which books to remove and, as before, the tapping came to an abrupt end.

Jack reached up to his Spiderwick series, deciding to pull out number two, *The Seeing Stone*. Before his fingers touched it, the book nudged forward—probably just a millimeter or two—by itself.

By its fourth movement, Jack was on his feet. What on earth was big and strong enough to move a book, yet small enough to fit behind one? The book moved again and now poked halfway out. There was no time to come to any rational decision of what to do. The book flew straight off the shelf and crashed to the floor.

Enough.

Without even a glance back in case something monstrous was flying after him, Jack bounded out of his room and virtually jumped down the two flights of stairs into the hallway.

Clinging to the banister and peering back up, he calmed a bit, knowing there was a safe enough distance between him and the bookcase beast. Jack took a deep breath in but, on exhaling, a dreadful realization swept over him.

Oh no! There was someone else in the hall. He peered over his shoulder.

Mom and Dad looked horrified. And beside them, the new neighbors wore their own shocked expressions.

"Son? Is everything okay?" Dad asked, a mixture of concerned and surprised tones in his voice. "Our guests have arrived." He tilted his bushy head in their direction.

Jack opened his mouth to respond when he noticed the three women staring, not at his face, but at his body.

In his crazy panic he'd forgotten he'd been in the middle of getting dressed. A chill spread through Jack's body. What underwear did he have on? Dare he look? He had to. He needed to know how bad this was.

Jack kept his head up while his eyes snuck a speedy peek downwards.

Disaster! Lime-green boxer shorts with black puppies.

A gift from Gran. Why did he choose today to wear these ones? Why not his skull and crossbones pair? Or the blue soccer pair? No. Without caring what he'd pulled from the drawer that morning, he'd put on the most childish pair he owned.

Now he understood why people wanted the ground to swallow them up.

"Hello." It was the young girl who spoke.

Jack's eyes darted up to her. She was pretty with a pale complexion and icy-blue, cat-shaped eyes. Right now her face was contorted, clearly trying to stifle laughter.

"Hi," Jack responded, sliding his arms down and spreading his fingers as wide as they'd go.

She looked him straight in the eye.

His cheeks were crimson, the burning sensation gave that away, and he could feel clammy sweat building in every pore. Was this really happening?

"I'm Roxy. Roxy Fox," she said, holding out her hand.

Jack paused. Raising just one arm would expose his scrawny body again and probably draw attention back to his underwear. But he knew he couldn't just stand and stare at Roxy's outstretched hand for much longer. Not without looking weird.

What a nightmare! Of epic proportions.

So, moving one arm diagonally across him, he held out his other hand and shook hers. Her skin felt warm and soft.

"Yes, yes of course," Mom said. "This is my son, Jack.

Jack, this is Roxy, as you now know, and Roxy's mother, Mira Fox," she continued, gesturing her hand in each of their directions.

Jack had forgotten how anxious he'd been about meeting Roxy's mother. The entire episode that morning had been squashed right to the back of his mind. He smiled thinly.

"Hi," he said again, unable to think of anything else to say.

A moment of silence followed.

Why wasn't anyone saying anything?

"Umm… okay… yes, let's go into the kitchen and have a cuppa!" Mom cried, throwing her arms up as if celebrating a goal she'd just scored. "I've baked a couple of delicious cakes to have with our tea. Yes, let's go there now and enjoy them, that *is* a good idea. Yes, come please, this way to the kitchen, yes this way." Mom nodded furiously with a strained, toothy smile stuck to her face.

While ushering her guests into the kitchen and talking incessantly, she threw a look at Jack as she passed. Wide eyes and flared nostrils: a look that told Jack exactly how she felt. However, a scolding from her couldn't make him feel any more ashamed than he already did.

When Mom, Mira and Roxy had left the hallway, Dad took a step closer.

"Everything all right, son?" he asked, placing a hand on Jack's shoulder, his warm, brown eyes staring right into Jack's.

"Yes, Dad," Jack replied, his hot cheeks beginning to cool down. "Everything's fine."

"Okay, son. Do you think maybe you should... well... you know... put some clothes on?"

"Yep, I should."

"Okay, see you in the kitchen." And with a reassuring tug on Jack's drooped shoulders, Dad smiled and followed the women.

Jack breathed freely again. Thank goodness that was over.

He now stood alone—and half naked—in the hallway. Could he ever get over this moment? But rather than wallow in the embarrassment, he sped to his bedroom. And once he was sure no monstrous insect was circling his room, he threw on the clothes he'd chosen earlier and joined the others at the kitchen table.

CHAPTER FIVE

THE ACTUAL FIRST VISIT

In the light of his headlamp Jack lay, staring at the
same sentence in his book over and over, Roxy's voice
in his mind.

Thankfully, the afternoon tea ended up going well.

First up, Mom had baked two very safe and tasty cakes:
a chocolate chip and custard extra-large muffin, accompanied by a banana and sultana cake topped with chopped
walnut sugar. Yum.

Second, Mira had been quiet, silent actually, barely
making eye contact with anyone. Weird behavior, yes, but
any ideas Jack had that she'd been looking at him through
the window earlier had been dispelled. He'd decided, po-
litely put, she was obviously a bit *different.*

And clearly she moved in such a stiff, unnatural fashion because of her ridiculous height. It didn't take long to
get used to.

What he couldn't get used to was her hair. Amazingly,
it was more white, curly and crazy close up.

But, most importantly of all, Jack had managed not
to embarrass himself any further that afternoon. Plus,

26

he'd found Roxy to be wicked company. Not only had he found it difficult to take his eyes off her, she was funny and smart as well. Climbing into bed that night, she was all he could think of.

Her voice buzzed around in Jack's head. His heavy eyelids drooped over his tired eyes and, as a satisfying slumber immersed him, his last waking thought was that maybe, just maybe, the rest of the school break would be interesting after all.

TAP! TAP! TAP!

Jack's eyes pinged open.

TAP! TAP! TAP!

The tapping was back, and it was much louder than it had been that afternoon.

TAP! TAP! TAP!

This time it was quickly followed by a bang, a shuffling sound, and then what Jack could only assume was something climbing onto his bed. His comforter was slipping away from him. He gripped it tightly and yanked it up to his chin. Adrenalin rushed through his body, and a panicked voice squeaked in his head. What on earth was in his room?

"Jack," a high-pitched whisper said.

Jack fixed his eyes on the ceiling and held his breath.

"Jack."

His top half flung forward as if controlled by a spring. His headlamp was still strapped on his head, and its urgent beam shone straight out in front. As his sight came into focus, he began to make out the owner of the voice standing on the end of his bed.

It was no bigger than one of Jack's stuffed animals and held its huge green hands up to hide its face from the light.

"The light! The light! Please turn it away!" it cried.

Without thinking, Jack removed his lamp and placed it onto his bed, and the light shone to the side of the creature. Two long arms dropped to its sides, enormous fingertips rested on the comforter.

Jack stared at its little round head. It had features like a human but very different. Its eyes were bigger, and its nose and mouth much smaller.

It just couldn't be real; Jack had to be in the middle of a dream. He wanted to rub his eyes but he couldn't remember how. And besides, if he looked away, it might attack him.

"Jack, it is a pleasure to meet you." The creature shuffled towards him. Little protrusions all over its head wiggled, then stopped, then wiggled some more.

Jack sat numb, watching what had to be a figment of his imagination. That weirdly knew his name...

Ignore it. It will go away.

The critter held out one giant hand as it now stood just inches away. Oh wow. Now it wanted to shake Jack's hand. But he couldn't lift either of them. All communication between brain and body had been lost, so he just stared at the huge green fingers in front of him and the thin red band that circled its tiny wrist.

"We come from Khloros to ask for your help."

"Khloros?" Jack asked, surprised that speech was still a fully working faculty.

"Yes, in your language, Khloros, a planet within a different solar system to Earth. I am a Freogan and my name is Freond," it replied.

"Life from a different solar system? That can't be," Jack said. Was he really conversing with an alien?

"Well, I can assure you it is true. There are billions of planets within our galaxy where life forms exist."

"Right. I just thought…" Jack couldn't finish the sentence. What *did* he think?

"I repeat, we are here to ask for your help," Freond said.

"Wait… we?"

"Yes."

And, as if in the middle of a bizarre dance routine, two more tiny, green heads popped out from behind Freond. One to the left and one to the right. Identical bodies followed. One wore a blue band around its wrist, and the other a yellow band. They were like friendship bracelets that all the girls in Jack's class wore. But girly or not, at least it was a way to identify each of them.

"Please meet Freond and Freond," the first Freond said as all three aliens bowed to one another and then to him.

Jack stared. Freond, Freond, and Freond. Three Freogans. Wearing friendship bands.

His eyes moved first to the right corner of his room, then to the left, checking for anyone else. Because, seriously, this had to be a prank.

"We need your help," continued Freond-the-Red—the name would do for now.

"My help?" Jack replied.

"Yes, your help. Something has been stolen from us, and we need your help to retrieve this item."

Jack pointed at his own chest. "Me?"

"Yes, you."

"Why me?"

"We have determined that the stolen object has coordinates of 9-4-6-3-5-5. You are the closest human."

"But I'm a twelve-year-old boy, I..."

"We have already studied you and believe you are ideal for our needs."

Jack gasped—the spaceship encounter! "What about the other kids that live nearby? Or my mom and dad?" he asked, not really convinced that being the closest human qualified him for such a task.

"We never trouble big humans, they think too much. You, Jack, are our chosen one."Freond-the-Red lowered its head.

Hallucinations. They had to be hallucinations. Talking ones.

"What am I supposed to find for you?" Jack said.

"Our Vitax. After many years of searching, we have

finally narrowed its location to here."

"What's a Vitax?"

"Something that protects our galaxy, Friend Jack. Something very important." The alien's eyes widened a little.

Jack wrapped his arms around himself. "Who stole it?"

"A group of aliens that live beneath the Earth's surface."

"A group of aliens that live beneath the Earth's surface?"

"Yes."

"Beneath the Earth's surface, near where I live?"

"Yes."

"Where? But when? Since when?" Come on, Jack had lived on Winell Road since he was born; it would be pretty obvious if an alien world was nearby, above or underground.

"We do not have all the answers at this time," Freond-the-Yellow said.

Jack shook his head. "So how can *I* get your Vitax back when I don't even know what it looks like?"

"The Vitax takes many forms, you will know it when you find it," Freond-the-Blue said.

"Why can't you go and get it back?"

"Freogans are not welcome and will be detected in their world, but humans are safe," Freond-the-Red said.

"What are these aliens going to do with your Vitax?"

Freond-the-Red leaned forward. "We have intercepted

messages that reveal they are due to exchange it for weapons from another galaxy ruler, but this is not the case. A dangerous alien gang leader is tricking them and will use it to destroy our star, then your star, and plunge us all into eternal darkness." The alien covered its face with one of its enormous hands, the other two flanking it copied. Jack waited, his gaze shifting from one to the next. After what seemed like minutes, Freond-the-Red separated two fingers and peered out from between them. "This must not happen. The Vitax being missing from its location is already causing the Milky Way severe unrest."

Jack looked from one Freogan to the next again. He was definitely being pranked. Three little green men with a story straight out of Hollywood. How should he play this? Maybe just go along with it.

"How do I know that *you're* not dangerous aliens?" A smart question; Jack's confidence had returned. He scanned the room for signs of a hidden camera.

"Because we are not," Freond-the-Red said.

Jack waited for more, but that seemed to be the end of the answer.

He shook his head. Saying he was confused would be an understatement. This was some prank. Who did he know that would do something this freaky? Or go to this much trouble. Maybe it was a dream, which, if true, was *the* most vivid one he'd ever had. But he felt like he was awake. Which left the final option—he wasn't well. Seriously not well.

"So you will help us?" Freond-the-Red moved his little head forward in search of an answer.

"Umm... well... I don't really know what to say," Jack replied. It was an honest answer but perhaps he should just say yes. None of this was real, so it wouldn't matter what he said, right?

"Please, Friend Jack, you are our only hope."

The aliens closed their eyes and lowered their heads in unison.

"I've got a question," Jack said, tapping a fingertip to his lips. Maybe he could trick them and regain control of the situation, whatever it was: dream, prank or hallucination.

"Of course, Friend Jack. What may your question be?"

"You travelled into Earth's atmosphere in a spaceship, right?"

The three aliens nodded.

"Well, surely this would have shown up on some NASA satellite thing somewhere. You can't be here without anyone else knowing, which means they will come looking for you, and probably me, for that matter. I could become a major NASA experiment and—"

"No one else knows we are here."

"That isn't possible."

"Our ship is made of a substance undetectable by your basic human machinery."

"But people, other humans, would have seen you."

"Humans only see us if we tap into their visual fields."

Tap into their visual fields? What did that mean? This was getting more insane by the second. Jack scratched his head.

The Freogans sat down on the bed. Freond-the-Yellow took over the explanations.

"Jack, there are many things you will not understand at this time. No book or TV program, no website or museum, not even what your Earthly leaders think they know comes close to the truth."

Freond-the-Blue continued. "There are many secrets, Friend Jack, billions of years old, which can never be known by everyone. These secrets keep us, you and me, safe. If they fall into the wrong hands... life as we know it would end."

"All you must know now is that we need your help to save our galaxy," Freond-the-Red said.

Now *that* was a sentence Jack had never expected to hear, not even in his wildest dreams.

"Without you, our mission can only fail. Please, we beg you."

Jack thought for a moment, staring at their peculiar but pretty friendly green faces. "What if I say no? You can go ask another human child, right?"

"Yes, but then we will have to terminate your life," Freond-the-Red said, his expression unchanged.

"Okay, okay, I'll do it!" Jack exclaimed, holding up his hands. On second thought, maybe they weren't so friendly.

"Thank you, Friend Jack. Thank you."

The three aliens rose to their feet and floated down from his bed. They bounced over to the bookcase like astronauts on the moon.

"How do I get underground?" Jack asked, swinging his feet to the floor.

"We have yet to discover how to access the world."

"How did you get in my room?"

"Zapage."

"Zapage?"

"Yes, Zapage. We set up a Zapage tube from our ship to your room. Our physical forms enter the tube and break down into Earth air particles as we travel through it."

Crazy! "How do you know about the internet and TV programs?"

"It doesn't take long for us to learn your primitive ways here," Freond-the-Red said.

After they'd climbed to the second shelf of the bookcase, Freonds Yellow and Blue nodded to Jack and disappeared into the books. Freond-the-Red stretched a hand towards the floor, and *The Seeing Stone* flew from the carpet and into the creature's palm. The alien gripped the book and backed up.

Jack shook his head. This really was too elaborate a joke—no one he knew could have pulled it off. So, if it wasn't a dream, he was clearly mental, and in that case he needed urgent medical help.

About to vanish, Freond-the-Red stopped with just its

head visible and gazed at Jack.

"There is something else you should know. Another creature is here looking for our Vitax. We don't know what or who this is, but they are not one of us. Be careful, Friend Jack. Don't trust anyone." The warning came just before the alien disappeared completely, the book sliding back into place.

Jack didn't waste a second. He vaulted from his bed and over to the bookcase. He snatched *The Seeing Stone* from the shelf, but all he found behind was the wooden bookshelf. No way!

"That can't be," he said, removing all the books and dropping them into a pile beside him. There was no hole or gap anywhere. He prodded the back of the bookshelf, hoping to find a loose section that the aliens may have opened like a doggie door—nothing.

On his hands and knee she crawled to the side of it and peered behind, squinting into the darkness—again nothing.

He leapt up, grabbed his discarded headlamp from the bed and dived back onto the floor. Shining the light behind the bookcase, he looked again. There was no hole in the carpet or baseboard. Moving the light up the wall, he saw no sign of any movement or marks that could've been made by anyone or anything, just plenty of thick dust and an uninhabited cobweb.

This made no sense. Where had they come from? And where had they gone?

36

Jack maneuvered his arm behind the bookcase, doing his best to avoid the web in case its eight-legged owner was loitering nearby. He attempted to lift the edge of the carpet so he could check for an escape route in the floorboards.

Suddenly, he felt something tickle his foot. Fumbling his way backwards, he shone the light at his bare feet.

A bigger pair of feet. And further up a pair of hairy knees, right by his nose.

"Aghhhh!" Jack cried, scrambling to his feet.

"Didn't mean to scare you, son. What are you looking for at this time of the night, well, morning? It's one thirty."

Dad! Jack brought his hand up to his heart and took some fast breaths. Of course, it was only Dad. Who else was it going to be?

"It's rather late to be reading if that's what you were doing." Dad raised an eyebrow and glanced at the pile of books Jack had ripped from his shelf.

"Yeah, yeah. I… I… I know." Jack moved past Dad and sat himself on the edge of his bed, his hand still pressed to his chest. It felt like an entire drum kit in there. "I remembered I had a book that Andy wanted me to mail to him over the break."

"Oh, right. So you keep that particular book *behind* your bookcase, do you?" Dad said, one corner of his mouth lifting.

Jack continued his fast thinking. "Well, no, of course

not. I'd put it on the top, and when I looked it wasn't there, so I guessed it had fallen behind."

"Ah, that makes more sense." Dad nodded. "What was the book called?"

"*The Alien Friend.*" It was the first thing that came to mind.

"I don't think I've heard of that one. Besides, it's a little late to be searching for a book. All the banging down here worried me. Perhaps get back to sleep now, eh, son? Maybe you can meet with Roxy tomorrow... after you've tidied up a bit. You seemed to be getting on well today." He raised both bushy eyebrows at Jack.

Resisting the burn in his cheeks, Jack nodded. "Okay, Dad. Sorry to wake you, I am pretty tired." Forcing a yawn and stretching his arms, Jack slid under his comforter and rested his head on his pillow.

His dad bent down, switched off the headlamp as he picked it up from the floor and popped it on the bedside cabinet. Ruffling his hand through Jack's hair, he smiled, said goodnight and left the room.

Listening to Dad climb the stairs, Jack lay quietly, waiting for the sound of the bedroom door shutting above him. He rolled onto his back, staring into the black.

He'd heard of crazy people who listened to voices but never ones who were visited by aliens. No, he wasn't sick, he was sure of that. And if Dad had heard him and could see the mess of books on the floor, then...

Jack felt suddenly like the smallest thing in the universe.

The Freogans had been real.

CHAPTER SIX

THE TRAPDOOR

The tummy-grumbling smell of frying bacon wafted under Jack's bedroom door and straight up his nose. He took a deep breath and smiled.

Normally, it would take him at least ten minutes to force his body out from the warmth of his blanket, but that particular smell always assisted the waking up process. That, and the growing realization that just hours ago he'd been visited by aliens asking him to save the galaxy.

With butterflies the size of soccer balls fluttering manically inside his stomach he scrambled out of bed, whipped off his pajamas and threw on some clothes—not forgetting a pair of simple plain, black boxer shorts. New motto: just in case. Full attention from that day forth would be paid to the style of underwear chosen.

Zipping up his hoodie, he squatted in front of the bookcase and started replacing the books he'd taken from the shelf last night. He rammed each book into the back panel in case he'd missed something. But no, it seemed pretty solid.

Last night's conversation played over and over in his head.

They said they'd chosen him simply because he was the closest human to their Vitax. For aliens who described Earth as primitive, they hadn't really put much effort into their selection process. It all seemed so unlikely to be real. It was impossible anyone lived on top of a world full of aliens—where humans were welcome—and didn't know about it.

After forcing the final book into the remaining gap, he splashed his face with water from his bathroom sink and bounded down to the kitchen. He felt far hungrier than most mornings, ravenous in fact.

Mom stood by the stove frying some eggs and bacon with a green, plastic spatula in one hand and removed two slices of toast from the toaster with the other. She dropped them on a plate and blew her fingertips.

"Morning, love," she said, smiling. "Good sleep?"

"Um... yeah, not too bad," Jack lied, salivating at the sight and smell of the food. "Is this for me?" He pointed to the toast.

"Yes. Pop some butter on... How many eggs?" Mom said loudly over the sizzling bacon.

"Three please, Mom."

"Hungry, eh?"

"Very."

Jack buttered his toast, and Mom served three eggs and three slices of bacon on top. He took a seat at the rectangular, wooden table at the far end of the L-shaped room and squirted ketchup into a neat blob on one side of the plate. And with a final deep breath, he dove in.

Mom joined him with her more modest helping of breakfast. Jack glanced at her across the table. Immediate conclusion, he couldn't tell Mom about last night. She'd probably faint or go into a frenzy if she thought he was on some kind of alien mission. Telling Dad was out of the question, too. Jack could see his face now: an expression that said: *my son is bonkers.*

"So..." Mom began, cutting her food into bite-size chunks, "...what do you have planned with Roxy today?"

"Dunno." It was the best he could manage through his mouthful.

"She'll be over soon. It's almost nine."

Swallowing, Jack tried to remember his last conversation with Roxy. "I don't think we arranged an exact time," he said, shoveling in some more bacon.

"No, but I told her that normally during summer break you were up at about eight-thirty so to come over at about nine," Mom said, concentrating a little too hard on the tiny piece of bacon she was cutting.

"Mom!" However, he wasn't wholly surprised by her interfering and tried to hide the grin creeping up his cheeks. He'd thoroughly enjoyed Roxy's company yesterday, not to mention his now burning desire to tell *someone* about both the spaceship and aliens in his room. He could trust her. She was the only remotely normal—and cool—person he'd ever met.

After wolfing the remainder of his breakfast and gulping his juice, he rushed back up to his room to brush his teeth. As he passed, he grabbed the remote and switched on his TV.

"We have some breaking news. Reports are coming in of some more strange activity... this time surrounding the planet Uranus."

With his toothbrush clamped between his teeth, Jack backed out of his bathroom until he could see the screen. The newscaster read from a piece of paper handed to him by an anonymous, pink-sleeved arm.

"This is now the final planet in our solar system to be affected by... unusual atmospheric activity. Experts say they can see... "— he glanced down at the piece of paper again—*"... significant changes to the surface of Uranus and numerous objects moving just above its surface."*

It was serious stuff. The man was using his most dramatic voice and occasionally glancing at his viewers over the top of his glasses.

"We will bring you more information on that story as it comes in." His face perked up and he removed his glasses. *"And now for the weather. Kelly, please give us good news. Is some much needed sunshine on the way?"*

A skinny lady with silky hair that reached down to her backside appeared on screen, posing beside a map of America. She threw her head back, laughing in a possessed-by-evil-demons style.

"I'm sorry, Bill, but no," she replied in the direction of the newsreader. *"I think the sun has been taken away by some aliens or something!"* She giggled and turned her almost or-

ange face towards the viewers at home. *"We've nothing but dark clouds and rain, I'm afraid. Maybe even some thunderstorms. Not much of a summer break for you kids, is it?"*

"Not much of a summer break, is it?" Jack copied in his best girly voice. He switched the channel, shaking his head. Another newscaster appeared.

"...like nothing they have ever seen before. Highly specialized equipment has been used to study Uranus and—"

Jack switched the channel again.

A NASA spokesperson was introduced. *"You can see here spherical objects bouncing up and down off the surface of Uranus. We've sped up the footage gathered here at our headquarters in Washington, D.C.. What we're seeing is similar to what some described as 'the beginning of the end', of course talking about last week's inverted tornado phenomenon seen all across the world."*

Inverted tornado? Jack must have missed that.

He changed channels.

A suited man appeared. The caption at the bottom of the screen labeled him as an official American Government spokesperson. *"We haven't yet discovered what is happening to these planets, but our top scientists are working on it as we speak."*

What a coincidence. Too much of a coincidence. Could it be possible there was a link between these reports, the spaceship and what the Freogans had spoken to him about last night? Mom's voice broke his thoughts.

"Jack! Roxy's here. I'll send her up."

Jack's heart pummeled his ribcage, and he sprang back

into his bathroom. Roxy arrived in his room before he'd even had a chance to put away his toothbrush.

While he wiped his face on a towel, he followed her out the corner of his eye. She plopped on the end of his bed and watched TV.

Had she said hello? Perhaps he hadn't heard. "Hi," he said, awkwardness always sending his manners into overdrive.

"Weird, eh, all this creepy stuff going on in space. I wonder if it's Armageddon," she said, leaning back and taking her weight on her hands as she crossed her long legs.

"Yeah, weird," Jack agreed, not really sure what Armageddon was and hesitant to let her in on his possible involvement just yet. "What would you like to do today?" Urgh, what a lame question.

"Dunno, what is there to do here?" Roxy shrugged.

A brainteaser. Jack didn't want to say *nothing* in case she thought he was boring but, at the same time, there actually wasn't anything to do.

He shot a glance out of the window. The rain, forecast by the lovely Kelly, hadn't arrived at Winell Road yet.

"Wanna explore the woods?" he asked, hoping she wouldn't find that a childish idea.

"S'pose," she said.

Relief. "Great. I'll throw a few things in my bag."

"What do you need a bag for?" Roxy asked, taking her eyes off the news report for the first time.

"Oh, err… just my phone… and stuff."

Jack wasn't actually sure why he did need a bag. Habit, probably. Most of the time he packed up a few bits to keep himself busy for the day because, ordinarily, no one accompanied him on his woodland adventures.

"Let's see your phone," Roxy said, holding out an expectant hand.

Jack lowered his head, already feeling the shame. He handed her the Codebreaker. She was bound to think it was stupid. She turned it over in her hands as he braced himself for all the pointing and laughing. "Cool," she said, giving it back.

Wait, what? She approved? Jack raised his eyebrows and put it in his backpack, along with his alien cards and a pack of tissues. Why he chose those items was a mystery, even to him.

"Ready?"

Roxy nodded, and Jack turned off the TV. They went downstairs and into the kitchen.

"Where's your mom? And your dad, where's he?" Roxy asked.

"Dad's down in the basement, I expect, and Mom could be anywhere." Jack led the way out into the backyard.

Despite the thick clouds, it was pleasantly warm. But rain was inevitable; you didn't have to be a weather reporter to work that one out. Jack walked across the lawn towards the forest entrance at the end of the yard. Roxy, however, wasn't following.

So far, she'd never shown much enthusiasm about anything. It was all sarcasm, shrugging, and rolling her eyes. But the yard seemed to be forcing expressions her face probably hadn't pulled in a long time, and her body seemed to lose its stiffness. She looked pretty amazing.

Roxy breathed in deeply and looked over at him. Jack swallowed quickly, averting his gaze. He couldn't help but feel sad for her. It was as if she'd never seen flowers before.

"Whoa!" she said. "This backyard is epic."

"You really think?" Jack said, clearing his throat. It was okay, but *epic* wasn't a word that immediately sprung to mind. Who wanted to spend all day looking at flowers and vegetables? They didn't exactly provide much entertainment.

Roxy continued to gawp, turning this way and that, a slight smile brightening her expression. She really was proving to be interesting. But just like that, she snapped out of her trance and pasted the pout back on her face. "Is your mom around?" she asked.

"Somewhere. She's usually in her greenhouse."

Roxy headed straight there. Jack waited outside.

Mysterious why she was so keen on finding Mom. A girl thing, presumably. And she was taking forever. What was with that greenhouse? It was like *Doctor Who*'s Tardis.

After a while, Roxy appeared at the door. "Shall we explore these woods then?"

Jack led the way to the end of the yard and into the vast expanse of trees.

*****

After ten minutes or so of trudging through soggy ground and over tree roots, Jack stopped to find his bearings. Roxy leaned back on the trunk of a giant oak tree and shoved her hands in her jeans' pockets.

Jack removed the Codebreaker from his bag and pushed the time button.

9:23

A record, surely. He'd managed to bore Roxy after just twenty-three minutes in his company. Yet if she only knew what he was involved in, she'd definitely be more interested.

He opened his mouth but paused. No, it didn't feel like the right time to blab.

"Wanna make a fort?" she asked, looking at him.

Jack frowned. "O-kay." That was unexpected. Good though, it gave him a chance to show off. After all, other than soccer fort building was his thing. They gathered a selection of sticks, leaves and rocks and piled them up beside a tree with an arching branch.

Jack glanced at Roxy. He was busting to tell someone about the aliens, but was she the right someone? How would she react? She'd either laugh at him, or totally believe it. It was a gamble. He bit into his bottom lip, and nodded. *Yep, here goes.*

"Roxy, do you believe in..."

He stumbled sideways as the ground started shaking; a gentle vibration at first but steadily increasing in intensity, a loud rumble accompanying it. Jack surveyed the ground, then circled, checking out their surroundings. Where was it coming from?

Within a minute, the pile of materials they'd made collapsed, and all around them leaves fell like rain, shaking loose from the trees. It could only mean one thing...

Earthquake.

"Roxy! What's happening?" Jack shouted over the noise.

He gasped as Roxy crashed to the ground, smashing her head on a rock. Blood stained her white hair and trickled down her forehead. Her eyes rolled shut.

Oh no! What was happening? Was she dead?

The ground continued to tremble. Harder. Faster.

Unable to keep his balance, Jack was thrown onto his back. Desperately, he grasped for something to latch onto. He located a large tree root poking out from the ground and yanked. It was stuck fast. His fingers wrapped tightly around it and, rolling onto his belly, he grabbed it with the other hand.

The ground started to sink underneath his body. Jack tried to wriggle away, bending his knees and pulling on the root as hard as he could. But it was no use. Like a trapdoor, an enormous hole opened up under him. "Aarrggh!" What was going on? Rocks, sticks, leaves, anything not secured in the earth slid into it and vanished.

Including Roxy.

"NOOOOOO!" Jack screamed as her limp body slid into the pit and vanished in the darkness. Tears dripped down his cheeks. He barely had time to take in the sight of horizontal trees still rooted in the muddy doors of the trapdoor but not collapsing into the giant hole.

And now, dangling over the abyss, he clung to his root.

His hands hurt. His arms ached. And he was starting to slip.

In a final bid to save himself, he removed a hand and clawed at the mud. It was no use—the ground was too soft, caking up his nails.

Swinging from one hand like a monkey, Jack peered into the bottomless pit.

The unknown.

As his grip failed him, he squeezed his eyes shut.

This was it. He was going to die.

CHAPTER SEVEN

THE DISCOVERY

Jack opened his eyes. Darkness.

And after a couple of squeezy blinks, still darkness.

He concentrated on his body.

He was lying flat on his front with something cushiony and soft under his cheek. It felt good, like his warm, morning pillow. Perhaps that's where he was, in bed. And he'd just had the most hideous nightmare. Falling was a recurring dream heaps of people had, he'd read that in a book once. Of course, he had to be in bed.

He inhaled a deep breath. And quickly coughed and spluttered it straight back out. The smell was unbelievable. Beyond bad. So thick he could taste it.

"Urgh! What is that?" Was Mom's egg and bacon from the morning to blame?

His voice echoed around him, bouncing off nearby surfaces and straight back into his ears. Plugging his nose, he pressed his other palm into the ground and pushed up. But the back of his head knocked into a hard, jagged surface.

"Ouch!"

One thing was clear: he was definitely *not* in bed.

Rubbing the golf ball growing on his head, he squinted and scanned around. A tiny stream of light leaked in from somewhere. His pupils gradually allowed enough in so he could make out a moss-like carpet beneath him and a narrow tunnel constructed of rocks. Where did it lead?

Jack gagged—the stench was unbearable. He had to escape from it and fast, otherwise there was a growing chance he'd be seeing his breakfast again. If he could find the source of the light then that might be his way out. He moved his head around as best he could in the confined space, his eyes working hard to locate the light's origin.

There! Down past his feet.

He shuffled backwards. Elbows back and push; elbows back and push. To relieve the aching in his arms, he forced his thoughts to wander.

Could he be dead? If he had just fallen through a gigantic hole in the forest, was there any chance he could've survived the impact? And Roxy! Oh no, he'd forgotten about Roxy. Maybe she was dead, too. He had to find out; after all, he didn't exactly feel dead.

His mind drifted back to the tunnel. The light was getting brighter. It had to be the end. Spurred on by possible escape, Jack sped up, imagining his soccer teammates cheering him on.

"Come on, Jack! You're going to make it! Come on!"

And with a final couple of pushes, his legs dangled out of

the tunnel.

He'd done it!

Now he needed to be careful. He couldn't see what was out there, so he lowered himself slowly, gripping the rocks on either side of the tunnel. He tapped with his shoe, feeling around for anything he could rest his feet on.

A ledge. He transferred his weight.

Jack glanced side to side. The ledge ran across a rock face. A rock face inside a cave. A vast cave. Stalactites dangled from above.

No way was he going to look down. Goodness only knew how high up he was, and rock climbing wasn't one of his known skills. To his right, he spotted a platform about six feet away. With his body hugging the wall, Jack focused. First, he secured his right foot, followed by his right hand. Then he slid. Right foot. Right hand. Slide. "Agh!" His foot slipped from its rock. Stony debris crashed to the base of the cave, and it was seconds before Jack heard it scattering.

He closed his eyes. That was a long, long way to fall.

Turning back was pointless; he was halfway between the tunnel and platform. He had to push on. Finding determination from deep within, he started again.

It felt like it took forever but, eventually, he made it. He secured a foot and threw himself with the remains of his dwindling energy onto the platform.

Sitting in a hunched-over heap and catching his breath, Jack could now see his surroundings. Where was he? The cave was indeed vast and disappeared into deep dark tunnels in all directions. Jack peeked over the edge of the platform. At the very bottom, maybe sixty feet down, he spotted a giant railway track running the entire base of the cave. Two silver, metal strips ran parallel through the center. It would have to be a whopper of a train to travel on it.

A murmuring broke the silence. Roxy? Jack dropped to the ground, making himself as flat as possible. Staying out of sight seemed the best plan just in case it was someone else—someone dangerous.

He peered toward a series of archways running along the railway track. A man and woman, deep in conversation and both carrying clipboards, emerged from one. They were rather similar in appearance. Short and tubby with perfect, ironed blonde hair and large, round glasses.

"I did tell him, but you know what he's like," the lady said.

"I know, but it's not up to us, Agnes. I disagreed from the day the boy was born, but we're their friends. We have to support their decisions," the man replied.

Weird, but both of them looked frighteningly familiar.

Absurd, of course. Jack had been through a lot in the past hour, so his mind must be all over the place. Even so, he'd seen them before somewhere, he was sure of it. On television, perhaps?

Their conversation continued. "You'll just have to have another word with him, Alan," Agnes said.

"I'll try, okay? Anyway, shall we fetch some Werks and The Spinner?"

"Indeed." Then Agnes made some odd shapes with her mouth, a squeaking and clicking emerging from it.

Before Jack had a chance to consider what she might be doing, or indeed what Werks and The Spinner were, both answers came in quick succession.

First, knee-high, purplish balls, about twenty in total, rolled out in an orderly line from the same archway as Agnes and Alan. They spread themselves out evenly along the side of the track as if waiting for the arrival of their train. Then harsh screeching filled the cave. Covering his ears, Jack screwed up his face as the train tracks moved. What emerged from the darkness of one of the tunnels left Jack in no doubt as to where he was.

Cruising along, just missing a few of the lower-hanging stalactites as it passed, was what looked like an enormous spinning top; jet black with a belt of oblong windows around its center. Once it reached the patiently waiting purple balls, it came to a stop and the screeching ended.

Now the balls came to life. Out sprang several spindly arms from each and three spindly fingers sprouted from these. The creatures clambered up and onto the spinning top, dispersing all over its surface. As their fingers made contact, massaging the bodywork as if checking for damage, purple electrical sparks sprayed out.

Agnes and Alan were watching, occasionally touching their clipboards.

A spaceship? Aliens? Underground?

It could only mean one thing: Jack had inadvertently discovered the whereabouts of the underground alien world.

This was immense. Strangely coincidental but immense nonetheless.

Before Jack had a chance to process the sheer enormity of the situation, something else caught his attention. From a platform on the opposite side of the cave, light flashed.

Was it torchlight? A reflection? His eyes fixed on the area, waiting to see it again. And there it was.

Could it be... hair?

"Roxy!"

CHAPTER EIGHT

THE PASSAGEWAYS

"Roxy!"
It was during this second call that Jack realized he now stood on his platform. Was there any chance they hadn't seen him?

No, Agnes and Alan were both staring up, the Werks no longer moving. His cover was blown. Now what?

Had Roxy seen him? He caught a glimpse of her disappearing into shadows.

He took a tiny step back. And another.

Jack looked over his shoulder; a passageway. Should he run? But what might be out there, waiting for him?

His eyes returned to Agnes and Alan. They were still staring at him. What were two humans doing in a world of aliens? He had to assume they were humans and probably dangerous. He waited to see who would make the first move. It was Agnes.

Her hand moved to her side and slid into the pocket of her white coat. There was no point waiting to find out what she pulled from it.

Not knowing where he was heading or what he was actually running from, Jack found himself whizzing through a series of connecting passageways. This time the walls and floor were made of a shiny metal. Tin? Aluminum? Who cared.

He skidded around corners and sprinted along straight sections. But despite having run for some time, Jack hadn't seen a single door to open or room to hide in. There was no way out of these endless corridors. He stopped, panting heavily. This was hopeless.

Once he could breathe a little more easily, he looked around. He ran his hands along the walls, searching for anything that may provide an escape route; hidden buttons or a gap that he could force open. He couldn't stay there forever. He'd been spotted, and someone—or worse, something—would be along soon. What they might do to him... well, that was too terrifying to contemplate.

That moment arrived sooner than Jack had anticipated. A hissing reached his ears from the direction he'd come. But not hissing. The louder it got the more it sounded like someone whispering. He listened hard. Something was moving closer. Sliding along through the passages.

HUSSSHHH!

Whatever was coming was unlikely to be human. It didn't sound it. Jack sped off in the opposite direction, adrenaline pumping through his body. Not caring which path he took, he ran, the ghostly sounds of his pursuer with him every step of the way. Reaching a curved bend, he slowed to glance over his shoulder. A dark shadow loomed around the corner—but a shadow darker than anything he'd ever seen. It spread slowly across the walls and ceiling, filling the entire passageway. What was this thing?

Jack gasped. If it was a shadow, whatever it belonged to would eat him alive.

Stepping up a gear, he continued running and, around the next bend, crashed straight into something.

"Oomph!" Jack fell back. He looked up, expecting hideous claws or gnashing teeth dripping with fresh blood, but instead it was the best sight he could've asked for.

"Jack!" It was Roxy looking flustered. "What's going on?" She reached her hand out to help him up.

"Now's not the time! We need to get out of here!" Jack cried, grabbing her hand and yanking her along behind him. "We're not alone."

"What?"

"We have to find a door, a way out. There's no time to explain."

"Wait, I found one, this way."

CHAPTER NINE

THE DOOR

Roxy took over the lead and, upon reaching a fork in the passageway, dragged Jack off to the right.

There it was—an ordinary-looking, wood-paneled door.

Running at full speed, they slammed into it and fell to the floor.

Clambering back to their feet, Roxy and Jack took turns trying the doorknob. It seemed to be broken. Or locked. Even wiggling it ferociously didn't make a difference.

Trapped in a dead end, the shadow creature spilled gradually across the walls towards them.

"Roxy, come on!" Jack screamed. "It's coming!"

He forced his body against the door and pushed with all his might. Roxy continued to fight with the handle.

Jack looked over his shoulder. The shadow changed shape and slithered closer. Black fingers stretched across the walls, inching nearer. They sharpened into blade-like claws and rose up, closing in on him. A menacing, high-pitched scream pierced the passageway.

With one last desperate shove, the door flew open. Jack

and Roxy leapt through together and slammed it shut.

Holding their breath, they listened, expecting tearing and scratching against the other side. But it didn't come. Staring wide-eyed at each other, they exhaled at the same time. Had they made it? Had they escaped imminent death—again?

Jack's body loosened up. And after a second or two to catch his breath, he glanced around.

They were in a dingy room. Piles of boxes, folders, files and loose papers were stacked up everywhere, hiding almost every inch of the exposed brick walls. His eyes moved to a lonely table in the center of the room with an assortment of tools on top. A rusty old hammer, a saw, several screwdrivers, and other utensils that he didn't know the name for, let alone how they could be used.

A mahogany desk was positioned beside the far wall, overflowing with piles of paperwork. Light from a table lamp shone down on a hand busy scribbling onto a piece of paper. The hand was attached to a man sitting at the desk.

Jack shook his head in complete bewilderment.

"Dad?"

The man turned and peered over his reading glasses, a smile breaking the concentration on his face.

"Jack," Dad said with a cheesy grin. "And is that you, Roxy?"

"Hi, Mr. Mills," Roxy answered.

Jack looked at her. She could see Dad, too. It wasn't

another one of his crazy hallucinations.

"What are you doing here?" Jack asked.

"Well, I'm working, son. This is my workshop... where I work. Perhaps I should ask you what *you* are doing here," Dad said, chuckling.

"Nothing!"

"Yeah, nothing," Roxy joined in. "I mean, not nothing, but Jack was just showing me round... you know... your house."

Good thinking.

"How wonderful," Dad said. "Is it raining yet? Maybe you should get outside before it does." He swiveled around in his chair.

"Great idea!" Jack agreed. "Come on, Roxy, you've seen Dad's workshop now. Let's head outside."

"Okay. Thanks for letting us look round, Mr. Mills," Roxy said. Jack noticed how uncharacteristically sweet her voice sounded. Boy, she was good.

"No problem. Have fun," Dad said without turning away from his work.

Jack walked as calmly as he could, Roxy right behind him, to the small staircase that led up to the ground floor. His thoughts were uncontrollable, his body shaking.

Exploding into the backyard, they ran deep into the trees, not caring that the first of the predicted rainfall had begun, until they could run no more.

"Oh my!" Roxy exclaimed, panting. "Did that just happen?"

"What part?" Jack said.

"All of it!"

"I think so."

"You realize, Jack, that under your yard and house is some secret underground world, don't you?"

"With a door leading straight into my basement."

"Yeah. What was that thing chasing us?"

Jack gulped. "I dunno. A shadow with claws that screamed."

"What do you think it was?"

Jack paused and looked at Roxy. It was time to tell her.

"Roxy," he said, "there's something you're gonna need to know."

"What?" she asked, her blue eyes sparkling.

"A few days ago, I had an encounter with a spaceship, and last night... well, some aliens from another solar system visited me in my bedroom. They asked for my help." He stopped to check out her reaction.

"Your help?"

"Yeah, I know it sounds a bit... well... unlikely, but they told me about an underground world. They asked me to get back something that was stolen from them and is now being kept there. The fact we've just found that world means everything else they told me is probably true, too."

Roxy's eyes grew wide. "Whoa! This is big. Massive. What was stolen?" she blurted.

Relief washed through Jack. She actually believed him.

"They called it a Vitax. They said it keeps the peace in the galaxy or something, and that since it's been gone, there have been problems."

She slapped a hand to her cheek. "Do you think those news reports about the other planets and the upside-down tornados have anything to do with this?"

"I do now."

"OMG, Jack, this is major."

"Yeah, I know. That world with dangerous aliens, it leads straight into my house." Jack tried to swallow the strange feeling in his throat. "Roxy, what if any of them try to get in? What if they already have?"

"Then we need to get down there quick."

Jack whipped his head up. Was she serious? He bit his bottom lip. "Back down there with that shadow thing?"

"Yep, back down where there are probably loads more shadowy things."

"And other terrifying aliens we haven't even seen yet."

Roxy didn't answer. Both of them stared at the ground in front.

The rain now fell heavily, slapping onto the leaves above them. Jack sat on an uprooted tree trunk. He ran his fingers through his hair and paused as he pushed the heels of his palms into his forehead.

"We need a plan."

Roxy joined him on the tree trunk. "Where do we start?"

"I dunno, but there was something else the Freogans

told me."

Roxy looked at him with interest. "Freogans?"

"The aliens," Jack said.

"Go on."

"They said there was something else here, a life form, looking for the Vitax, and I got the impression it wasn't anything friendly either."

"So it's a race, too?"

"It seems that way."

They sat in silence, looking at each other.

Roxy stood suddenly, placing her hands on her hips. "Let's get home. We definitely don't want to make our parents suspicious right now."

Jack glanced up at her towering above him. "What are you thinking?"

"Tonight. We go back down tonight, through your basement door."

Jack's insides flipped over.

"We've got to take this seriously, Jack. The whole world could depend on us."

Jack remained seated and nodded slowly.

A clap of thunder rumbled in the distance. The magnitude of the situation hadn't reached him, until now.

CHAPTER TEN

FIRST SUSPICIONS

They decided to go back at midnight. Jack would let Roxy in through the back door and they'd go to the basement together. In the meantime back in his bedroom, he needed to create some sort of plan. Any sort of plan.

Pacing, sitting, lying, sitting back up, standing, staring out the window, pacing again. Not one single position assisted with plot devising.

Complicated wasn't the word. Something kept revolving round and round in his mind.

How come Dad hadn't heard them smash through that door? A door that Jack never knew existed. The only explanation was the underground world wasn't actually underground at all, but rather the basement door was a portal to a whole new dimension. If it wasn't... Jack had no idea how to finish the sentence. Dad was Dad. Arthur Mills: inventor. Deep down, Jack just couldn't believe his dad would know about the other world.

He shook his head and slumped on the end of the bed. He looked at the display of screwed-up, scribbled-on notepaper littering his carpet like huge snowflakes. It was no use; his brain wasn't playing ball. He would have to ask Dad about that door some other time.

Jack sniffed—and cringed. He stank. Remnants of the tunnel stench were hanging around. He couldn't figure out if it was on his clothes, in his hair or simply loitering up his nose. He had to shower. For one, it would kill some time, but most importantly it might give his nasal passages a break.

Ten minutes later, a sweeter smelling Jack headed out the front door, cradling his soccer ball. The rain had eased, and he'd developed claustrophobia stuck in that bedroom.

Winell Road was quiet as usual. Jack looked at the sky. No spaceships around today—not yet anyway. He balanced the ball on one foot before chipping it up and over to the other, a skill he'd mastered years ago, but, today, he couldn't do it.

"Jeez!"

The ball bounced and rolled away in the direction of Petula's. Jack growled at the ground and stomped through the puddles after his ball. He hated mucking up soccer tricks.

In front of Petula's house, he peeked in the window and awaited the familiar grimace, but, oddly, Petula's head didn't pop up. Unusual. She'd be in her element right now, what with Jack being so close to her house. He tried the next window. No scowl there. And the next. Again nothing. Where was she?

Jack stepped back, admiring Petula's home.

He'd nicknamed it The Die because of its appearance: one level, perfectly square, flat-roofed, painted white with black-framed windows on three sides and an overly large, black door on the fourth. Completely different to all the other houses on Winell Road. And its location, right by the street's entrance pillars, was seriously convenient considering how nosy Petula was.

Then there were the other houses: was it possible they had exactly the same layout as his house? All of them with basements and secret doors that led into underground alien worlds. Why wasn't there a number 1? Why did the houses start at number 2?

He began to examine each house with a completely new mindset, his eyes moving to number 2.

All these years and he'd never wondered why a car would be parked on the driveway of an empty house. Why hadn't he? Both cars were shiny and clean. Surely if they *were* abandoned, like Dad had told him they were, they'd show some sign of this: fallen leaves on the hood, rust around the edges of the doors, dirty glass, and perhaps some splattered bird poop. But no, they appeared brand new. Like they always had. And that could only mean one thing: someone must be looking after them.

His mind returned to his first thought.

Where was Petula? *Who* was Petula? He'd accepted all his life that she, like the other residents of Winell Road, was simply a peculiar character, eccentric even, nothing more. But now it just didn't seem feasible that every house on this street was occupied by oddballs—oddballs who made even his parents seem normal. And strange that such oddballs just so happened to live on a street with an alien world below its surface.

His breathing sped up a notch. Could they all be aliens? If this was true, how the heck had his mom and dad ended up living here?

No, what a stupid thought. And besides, Mom often visited Mrs. Atkins and never mentioned anything out of the ordinary about her. Other than her flower obsession.

But the more he thought about it, the more it seemed possible.

Petula and George were creepy-looking humans, and the family at number 8 was highly unusual—Mrs. Fann and her tiny, identical octuplets. Who else could boast of a family like that living nearby? Not many people, for sure. But the mini Fanns were just children, younger than him. There was no way they could be aliens... or could they? *He'd* just become embroiled in a galaxy-saving mission, so surely anything was possible.

Jack shook his head. He was going mad. Quite mad. He'd grown up here for goodness' sake. He knew these people. But did he? What did he actually know about them?

Jack turned slowly around. If his neighbors were from the underground world, then they had to be involved in the stealing of the Vitax—and he'd been spotted down there. They could be on to him, watching him right now.

Jack could hear his fast breathing, but his panic soon broke at the sound of his mother's voice.

"Dinner!"

Not wanting to jeopardize his plans with Roxy, Jack picked up his soccer ball and hurried back home. No way did he want to arouse any worry or suspicion in his parents. No, it was crucial he carried on as normal. He had potentially put them in as much danger as he was. As he passed, he glanced over at Roxy's house, at the third window up. Was her bedroom on the same floor as his? There was no sign of life there.

A movement. His eyes shot down to the front door. His sneakers scuffed as he stopped dead.

Mira.

Her black eyes bore into his skull. How long had she been there, watching him? The curtain twitched upstairs. Roxy? Had she been trying to get his attention? Was she okay?

The front door slammed. Mira vanished.

What was going on?

Mira spooked him.

Winell Road was starting to spook him.

He rushed indoors, his head pounding.

CHAPTER ELEVEN

MORE SUSPICIONS

"You had a good time with Roxy today, then," Mom said, pulling out a chair at the kitchen table.

Cutting up his pork chop, Jack composed himself. He couldn't give anything away.

"It was okay."

"Just okay? You seemed to be getting along when you came down to the basement," Dad said with a wink.

"You were in the basement?" Mom asked, several frown lines creasing her forehead.

"Oh yeah... umm, Roxy wanted a tour so I showed her around."

"Yes, they seemed to be having a great game."

"It wasn't a *game*, Dad, we were looking around." Roxy was thirteen, she didn't play games. So when Jack was with her, neither did he.

"Of course. Of course. So what else did you do?"

"Wandered about in the woods... and stuff." He quickly filled his mouth with food.

"Right, well, I suppose that's what kids do these days,"

Mom said. "And tomorrow, are you seeing her tomorrow?"

"Maybe," Jack mumbled. Didn't they have anything else to talk about?

A few uncomfortable, silent minutes passed.

"How was Mrs. Atkins today?" Dad finally asked Mom, and Jack released a breath.

"Same as usual. Cross with me because I was one minute late with her flowers and because she couldn't have more," Mom replied.

"Why can't she pick her own flowers?" Jack paused and looked up. The question had just come out. Too quick to stop.

"She can't walk very well, and anyway, it's nice my flowers go to good use," Mom replied with a shrug.

"What does she do with so many?" Oops, and there was another.

"Where are all these questions coming from, Jack?"

"It's only my second question. I'm just curious."

"She eats them." Mom rolled her eyes.

Dad chuckled. "Ha! Good one, love!"

Jack narrowed his eyes. Mom seemed a bit touchy. No more questions for her. He switched his attention to his dad. The flow had started. He needed answers, and now seemed as good a time as any.

"Dad, that door in the basement, where does it go?" He braced himself for the answer.

"What door, son?"

"The one over in the corner, I've never noticed it before." He slid a potato around his plate with his knife.

"Oh, that's an empty old cupboard. To be honest, Jack, I lost the key years ago."

Jack studied Dad's face. No, he wasn't lying; Dad had no idea what was really behind it. And, knowing how caught up he got in his work, he probably had forgotten about it anyway.

"That's enough questions, Jack." Mom still appeared irritated. "Eat up. You'll need your strength so you can finish building that fort tomorrow."

Jack stopped, his fork hovering halfway between his mouth and plate. He stared at his mom. "What fort?"

"The one in the woods."

"How do you know about the fort?"

"You mentioned you wandered in the woods and started building a fort." She wasn't looking at him.

"I didn't mention a fort." Jack lowered his fork. It hit the plate with a loud chink.

"You did just then, you mentioned a fort."

"No, Mom, I didn't."

"Oh, well, it's what you normally do when you go out in the woods. I must have just imagined you said it." She stood with her plate of half-eaten dinner and scraped the food into the trash.

Jack's appetite evaporated. He felt sick.

*****

72

Lying on his bed, Jack looked over at his clock.

10:30 P.M.

An hour and a half to go before their mission, but his mind was elsewhere.

How could Mom have known about the fort he and Roxy were going to build unless she'd been there? Okay, she was nosy, but if she'd been spying then she would've seen them fall into the hole.

Yet her behavior didn't exactly point to a mother whose child had fallen down a giant hole. Wouldn't she be panicked or relieved he was alive? Maybe she really had guessed they were going to make a fort. He thumped his palm into his forehead. His thoughts were out of control. Since when had Mom been anything other than a hideous cook? Why was he finding her conduct suspicious all of a sudden? It was his mother, wacky old Mom, for goodness' sake.

And Dad, how could he have suspected Dad? But Fre-ond-the-Red's last words kept running through his head...

Don't trust anyone. Did that include his parents? Surely not.

"Ergg!"

It came from the bathroom.

"Oooo!"

What was that? Another alien?

"Pull!"

Jack froze. Should he leave quietly before whatever it was knew he was there?

"Ow!"

Leave and go where? Where was safe? No. He was braver than that. It was time to summon courageous Jack to the room.

He crept towards the bathroom door and, pushing it open, saw something moving behind the frosted glass of his shower screen. *Three* things moving. Three *green* things. Jack stepped closer and peered into his shower.

"Argh!"

Freond-the-Red. And it seemed to have one of its giant toes stuck in the plughole. The other Freogans were yanking at its leg.

And they said humans were the primitive ones.

"Friend Jack! Please help me," Freond-the-Red said.

"Why didn't you come through the bookcase like before?" Jack asked. He bent down and wiggled its toe from the plughole. It felt rather similar to a human toe, smooth and warm.

"It is important for me to move the entrance to your room as often as possible. We are not the only species that uses Zapage to travel. If found, our tubes could be penetrated at any part."

Great! Now there was a chance any old alien could drop by for a surprise visit.

With a final pull and wiggle, Freond-the-Red's toe popped out from its trap.

"Thank you, Friend Jack. I will avoid this entrance in future."

"Good idea," Jack agreed.

The four of them filed into Jack's bedroom.

"You have found the alien world," Freond-the-Red said.

Jack sat on his bed and stared at the alien. "How do you know that?"

"We know because we are following your every move."

Every move? Even when he... No, that would be silly.

"We have sensed there is a problem, Jack," Freond-the-Yellow said.

Jack looked at them, not really sure what to say. "No... I mean yes, there is. I don't know. Everything around me is different all of a sudden—my home, my neighbors, my parents... I think that... well, I thought that... I'm wondering if..." He quickly wiped away a tear before it had the chance to leave his eye.

"Friend Jack, please don't be afraid," Freond-the-Red said.

"I'm not afraid, it's just... "

"If you were, it would be a normal reaction to your current situation, but it is good to question life around you, to question yourself."

"But my own parents?"

"Yes indeed. They are your rock, your constant, but even they must be questioned at times."

Jack didn't know how to respond. Was Freond-the-Red telling him he *should* be suspicious of Mom and Dad?

The Freogans moved to either side of Jack and sat down, each placing a giant hand on his arms. Jack glanced at their faces, a feeling of calm radiated through him.

"We are with you every step of the way, Friend Jack," Freond-the-Blue said.

"Yes, you are never alone," Freond-the-Yellow added.

"We are your friends," Freond-the-Red said. "Come, we must ensure the plan runs smoothly."

All three aliens rose to their feet and headed for different parts of the room.

One lifted Jack's alarm clock, analyzed it, and tossed it to one side.

The second prodded Jack's camera, before discarding it and diving headfirst into his clutter box.

"What are you doing?" Jack asked, his eyes switching to Freond-the-Red.

"We must find a way of communicating with you," it said before disappearing into Jack's backpack. It crawled out bottom first, clutching the Codebreaker. "This will work," it announced, admiring it closely. "With this we can contact you with valuable information. Can you see faces on here?"

"Faces? What do you mean?"

The Freogans huddled together, admiring the phone.

"Our investigations into the other life form searching for our Vitax are continuing. When we have discovered its identity, we can inform you."

Jack understood. "Ah, like a photo. Then yes, I can receive images on here."

"This is what I shall use." Freond-the-Red held the

Codebreaker close to his face. Its eyes rapidly flickered back and forth until the phone bleeped.

"It is now prepared for our image. Keep it with you at all times."

Jack took the phone and studied it, not really sure why he was expecting it to be any different.

"Friend, you have not told anyone about this mission, have you?" Freond-the-Red asked.

"No," Jack lied. Best to keep Roxy out of it. But if the Freogans were watching his every move, why weren't they aware she'd fallen into the alien world too? Odd.

"Good. Suspect everyone, Jack. We have sensed the life form is close."

The Freonds nodded their goodbyes and sprang back to the shower cubicle. One by one, they swirled down the plughole like dirty water.

At least none of them got stuck leaving.

Jack leaned against the doorframe of his bathroom and stared at the empty shower.

Not only did he have to recover this Vitax, when he still had no idea where it was being kept, but now he had to look over his shoulder at all times. He'd heard them—the life form was close.

The race was on.

CHAPTER TWELVE

BACK UNDERGROUND

Tick. Tick.

The passing seconds seemed to be slowing down again. Jack shook his clock for the millionth time, just in case it *had* stopped working.

Tick. Tick.

No, it was still fine.

And finally, the numbers flicked to 00:00.

That remaining hour had been stressful. Jack's nerves had taken a battering. Particularly with Dad's late finish, but thank goodness he hadn't worked through the night like he often did.

At 11:48, Jack had heard him climb the stairs and pause briefly outside Jack's bedroom door—as he always did. At which point, Jack adopted a been-asleep-for-hours pose— hand dangling over the side of the bed, mouth catching flies—on the off chance Dad poked his head round the door. But it wasn't necessary, Dad just continued up to the top floor.

It was time.

Codebreaker in hand, Jack cracked his bedroom door

and listened.

All was silent.

He wedged his head between the door and the frame and peered into the darkness.

All was still.

Mom and Dad must be tucked into bed. Now was his chance.

With ninja mode switched on, off he went. Although athletic, Jack wasn't exactly twinkle-toed. Mom would often ask him if he had an elephant in his room. So, as lightly as he possibly could, he tiptoed down the stairs, rehearsing his excuses in his head. *What you are doing?* I'm just getting a drink. *But why are you fully dressed?* I fell asleep with my clothes on. *But you have your shoes on...* Darn! He should've thought things through more thoroughly.

Jack needn't have worried—he made it, unnoticed, to the kitchen. Outside the kitchen window, Roxy was already waiting. He unlocked the door and let her in. Without speaking, they nodded a greeting and headed down the final staircase into the basement.

They weaved their way through the piles of Dad's work, taking extra care in the virtual blackness. If just one paper skyscraper went over it could be disastrous, spelling the end. They opened the cupboard door, the ominous metal passageway beckoning them in.

Jack shivered. What if the shadow thing was loitering around the corner?

"Wait!" Roxy hissed, snapping Jack from his fear.

He turned as she picked up a triangular piece of wood from the floor and wedged the door open, just enough so there'd be none of that horrible panic fighting the door on their return. What a brilliant idea! Jack's shoulders relaxed a touch.

They reached the end of the first passageway and, with the basement door still visible behind them and no shadows up ahead, Jack spoke in a low voice. "We need to be able to find our way back here easily. These passageways are like a maze, and if we end up being chased again I don't want to get lost."

"Okay, we should leave some marks, then," Roxy said.

"But at the same time, we definitely need to keep them visible only to us. The last thing we want is to lead any aliens straight into Dad's workshop."

"Erm... we could scratch into the metal walls?" Roxy suggested.

"Good idea. Do you have anything sharp we can use?" Roxy patted herself down. "Not on me."

"Me neither. What about a pen? Maybe we can draw on the wall or the floor."

"Well, a pen wasn't on my *to bring* list," Roxy said with an eye roll.

"Hang on!" Jack reached into his pocket and pulled out the Codebreaker. "Dad put this stupid pen in my phone." He pressed a button making a pen tip urgently shoot out from the top, startling Roxy. "If I draw something on the wall it will be invisible until"—he pressed another button and a thin beam of light shone out—"I shine this light on it."

Jack demonstrated by drawing and lighting up an arrow pointing toward the door.

"Whoa! Cool!" Roxy said.

They turned and began their journey.

As to where, Jack hadn't a clue.

*****

After turning many corners, deciding on many directions, and drawing untold numbers of invisible arrows, Jack stopped.

"Can you hear that?" he whispered.

"What should I be listening for?" Roxy replied, crouching down so her head was the same height as Jack's, her chin resting on his shoulder.

"Sshhh." Jack focused.

A gentle buzz, similar to the sound of a bee, gradually got louder.

"There," Roxy said, pointing. Jack saw it too.

Moving in their direction was… a head. A large swollen head that appeared to have been made from poop-colored Play-Doh, hovered just above the ground. Hundreds of tiny white wings where ears would normally be flapped ferociously, propelling it along.

Jack stretched out his bottom lip. The creature was grotesque. All of its eyes, five or six at a glance, opened and closed with a squelch.

Luckily, it didn't look like it had spotted them—a little strange considering all those eyes.

The hideous head cruised past them, gliding around the bend at the end of the tunnel.

"Phew." Roxy wiped invisible sweat from her forehead. "That was repulsive."

"Let's follow it," Jack said.

Keeping a safe distance behind, they followed the head, weaving their way around bend after bend, Jack carefully marking an arrow with the Codebreaker pen at each one. Finally, after considering whether the alien was actually just out for a leisurely fly, they arrived at its destination.

From under a large, stone archway, carved with symbols like nothing Jack had ever seen, he and Roxy looked out into a huge open space, as big as a soccer pitch. A raised walkway stretched around the entire perimeter, with several sets of stairs leading down to what seemed like some kind of central control room. The place buzzed with movement and sounds.

Jack's mouth hung open. Hundreds of species of aliens were going about their business, humans dotted amongst them. Some studied transparent images hanging in mid-air; some disappeared whilst others appeared through lights beamed in from holes in the ground; others vanished into tubes that stretched from the floor upwards, while new aliens exited other tubes.

As Jack watched, something troubled him.

Crazy as it sounded, even in his head, some of the aliens looked familiar. It was the same feeling he'd had when he'd seen Agnes and Alan. And here it was again. Recognizing humans was one thing, but aliens? Why? He did watch a lot of TV, so maybe he was staring at the set of some science fiction program. Or film. It was all very *Men In Black*-ish.

Maybe Roxy would know. Jack peeled his eyes away from the bizarre scene and looked across the archway.

Roxy had a look of complete astonishment stuck to her face.

But her eyes were fixed on one spot.

CHAPTER THIRTEEN

THE PILLARS

"Roxy? What are you looking at?" Jack said.

"Over there, Jack, do you see that? Odd place for a heavily-guarded door, don't you think?" She pointed a long, slender finger.

Jack followed her finger. Yep. It was indeed some door she'd found; fifty times bigger than any in his house. Strange thing, though, it didn't appear to be attached to anything. No walls above or behind, nothing to the sides. It was just a massive door in the middle of this vast room.

He squinted. Carved into the metal were symbols, like the ones on the archway. What were they? They looked like Chinese characters or hieroglyphs. Could it be alien writing?

But Roxy was right; two enormous stone statues, almost as tall as the door, were positioned side by side in front of it. Though it was doubtful they were just statues. Their rectangular heads were over half their size, and two golden slits for eyes sat either side of an elongated, huge-nostriled nose. Stone arms were held behind their backs. They reminded Jack of something out of ancient

84

Egypt.

"I'm going to bet my life there's something important behind that door," Roxy said, nodding slowly.

"Worth being guarded by two enormous aliens," Jack agreed.

"Like a Vitax, maybe."

This had to be the place. They must've found its location. Jack squeezed his hands into fists. "Now comes the hard part."

"Mmmm, how the heck do we get through it?" Roxy said.

"For starters, how do we get over there?" Jack scratched his head. "This place is crawling with aliens, and I've already been spotted once. We've got to take extra care it doesn't happen again."

"We're going to have to find an alien that we look similar to and try to copy it," Roxy said.

Jack waited for the punch line to Roxy's dreadful joke, but there wasn't one. Clearly she was serious.

"Are you for real?" Jack said.

Roxy, however, was already searching for her lookalike.

She'd gone insane! What a crazy idea. Stupid. And one that would unquestionably get them caught. But at the same time, Jack had nothing better to put forward. He needed time to think.

Too late. Roxy stepped onto the walkway.

"No, Roxy!"

It was no use. She was off.

Quick, he had to find something to copy. He scanned the ocean of aliens and spotted a gray one about his size. Slightly hunched over with two arms flopped by its sides, the alien skulked forward dragging its feet behind, with a real zombie-crossed-with-spoilt-teenager thing going on.

A possibility—until it produced three more heads from its body, and each one appeared to talk to the next.

Jack screwed up his face. "Ergh! Gross."

Roxy was now a fair distance from him, travelling in an extraordinary sideways fashion, her bottom sticking straight out.

Jack needed to catch up to her, so he chose to use the very human crouching-down method. It had worked for him in the past. Perhaps never in a situation quite like this, but it was all he had. He put up his hood and, moving at the quickest speed he could while keeping low, he ducked into any shadow that came along.

With just three feet separating him from Roxy, Jack slowed as something sticky attached to his shoe. He looked down. Had something spilled? Lifting his foot, a slimy, thick substance stretched up with it before pinging back to the ground. Crouching lower, tiny worms poked out from it, flapping back and forth like tongues. The goo was alive, whatever it was.

Jack reached forward to touch it, but the worms sank into the floor. At the same time, an ear-piercing siren rang out in the room. Everywhere darkened, orange lights flashed intermittently.

Had he been seen? He looked back to the floor. By the sticky stuff?

Jack searched for Roxy for an escape plan, but she was nowhere to be seen. Had she abandoned him?

Still in his crouched position, he curled himself into the smallest ball his body would allow, sinking his head deep into his shoulders. But after almost a minute of squeezing his eyes shut and hoping he'd somehow magically turned invisible, no one, or thing, was coming for him.

Through the bars of the walkway barrier, he watched aliens disappearing one by one into the giant tubes. Image screens were imploding.

Something serious was happening and, if it was enough to make hundreds of dangerous aliens scarper, then he had to get out of there too. And fast. Keeping out of sight remained a sensible idea, so Jack waited for his chance. When it came, he ran over to one of the tubes. Copying what the aliens had done, he stepped inside and, standing tall, prepared for lift off.

Of course it wasn't going to be that easy, what was he thinking? A small screen appeared on the inside of the tube. Jack waited for it to do something, but nothing happened. Did it need instruction from him? Perhaps he should speak.

He thought for a moment. "Begin." Nope, the screen remained lifeless.

"Go now!" The same.

"Move!"

"Up!"

"Start!"

Each attempt failed. What did he have to say? What other commands were there?

This was no good, he'd have to try his luck and get back out there, to the archway and through the tunnels.

Jack reached up to remove his hood, and at the same moment a bleep filled the tube. He lowered his hands and peered at the screen. Had it come from there?

Then it hit him. That bleep—the Codebreaker had made the same noise after Freond-the-Red had fiddled with it.

Jack gripped the phone and shoved it up to the screen. It bleeped again, and its display came to life. Numbers, letters and symbols whizzed all over, and after several seconds the display slowed down until just six numbers lingered, bouncing around the screen.

Having not a clue what it meant, Jack read them out loud.

"Nine-four-six-three-five-five."

From inside the tube, a female voice replied. "Hello. Speak your destination."

Jack's body jolted.

Whoa! Had the Codebreaker just broken into the tube's controls? Things were getting weirder by the minute. Dad said he'd found the massive mobile somewhere. Where? If it had been nearby, was it possible it belonged to the underground world?

With a deep breath, Jack tried a command. "Outside!"

The control room instantly faded away, as if a pair of black curtains was being drawn around him. But no sooner had the curtains closed than they reopened. It couldn't have worked. Maybe he'd been detected.

But instead of seeing flashing lights and hurrying aliens, a misty view of trees appeared in front of him. Stepping forwards, cold raindrops tickled his head. His warm breath hung in the air. Jack looked up to see a nighttime sky lit dimly by a cloud-covered moon. He'd definitely been taken outside. But where?

He tightened his grip on the Codebreaker as he squinted through the rain, looking for clues. Turning slowly around, he saw that the escape tube was no longer there. In its place stood a tall tree trunk, but, as Jack reached out to touch it, the bark felt too smooth to be a regular tree.

With one small step back, he gazed up, following the wood to the top. The full picture came into view. Jack looked over his shoulder, and there stood another smooth tree trunk.

But neither were trees.

He was standing between the two wooden entrance pillars to Winell Road.

"No. Way." He'd been teleported above ground. Two pointless pillars he'd passed every day for years had now become another gateway to an underground world.

His mind quickly returned to Roxy. She was still down there. What if she'd been captured? Or worse? What had he been thinking, leaving her down there alone? He had to get back to help her.

Searching for a way back into the pillar, he moved the Codebreaker all over its surface, waiting to hear the bleep as before. But he seemed to be out of luck. Maybe the pillars were only a way out.

Jack raced to his house.

*****

The basement door was still wedged open with the piece of wood Roxy had put there. Jack bent down and removed it, careful not to make a sound and wake his parents. Holding on to the doorknob, he nervously opened it wider.

A light shone at him from the other side of the basement. Jack turned his head in surprise, dropping the piece of wood, and looked straight into it, which instantly blinded him.

"Ouch!" His eyes burned, and he rammed his fists into them.

"Jack? Is that you?"

"Dad?"

The light moved away. Jack squinted at the outline of his dad halfway down the basement staircase.

"What are you doing down here at this time of the morning?" Dad said.

He was usually a calm man, but now Jack sensed his

dad was anything but.

"I'm starting to worry about you and your night-time antics. Now get over here."

Jack obeyed straight away. He listened to the basement door click shut as he released his grip. His heart weighed heavily. Roxy was imprisoned. He'd abandoned her.

With white blotches blocking his vision, Jack maneuvered back through the obstacle course of a basement.

"Jack, this is the second time I've caught you sneaking around in the middle of the night. If there's something going on, then I want to know about it."

They returned to the kitchen. Dad stood, hands on hips, head thrust forward, hair all over the place.

"You frightened me, I thought we had burglars. Thank goodness your mother hasn't woken. You know how she worries." His voice had calmed, but the rest of him hadn't.

Jack's mouth opened, but no words emerged. He was sorry, of course he was, but his mind was fixed on one thing—Roxy, stuck down there, all alone.

Jack's sullen face glanced up at his father, but, in the background, he caught movement through the glass of the kitchen door. Looking past Dad into the yard, he saw Roxy. She smiled and wiggled two thumbs-up at him.

She was okay.

Anxiety whooshed from Jack's body as if he was a deflating balloon. His legs felt like they'd transformed into marshmallows.

With his hands on his hips, Dad still waited for a response.

"I am *so* sorry, Dad. Really, I... I came down for a drink and thought I heard noises in the basement too and came to investigate, and then you appeared. Seriously, I'm not up to anything, I promise. Trust me. I'll do some extra jobs for Mom tomorrow to make up for worrying you." Fingers crossed he hadn't gone over the top.

"Well, okay, but please don't let me catch you out of your room at night again. And really, do you have to get dressed to get a drink in the night? Tennis shoes, too?"

Whoops!

"Night, Dad." Jack ran up the stairs, two at a time.

What a night! 3:04 A.M. Three hours of utter madness.

They'd done it, they'd located the Vitax. The Freogans would be thrilled. Now he and Roxy just needed to get back down there and through that door. It would be tricky, but they were one step closer.

One huge step closer.

And the Codebreaker, the most useless phone in the world, had become an unexpected asset. If only Dad knew what he'd found.

Changing into his pajamas, Jack didn't have an ounce of sleepiness in him. He couldn't wait to meet up with Roxy tomorrow. Was she as excited as him? They had so much to talk about, to plan.

It was really happening.

CHAPTER FOURTEEN

WINELL ROAD

After plenty more sucking up and a few more apologies, Jack wolfed down a huge bowl of oatmeal with honey. Time to find Roxy. They had so many things to discuss. How did she escape from the alien world? Where did she disappear to when the alarm rang out?

It was a cloudy morning, the ground damp from last night's rain, but there was a fresh clean smell in the air.

Jack inhaled a deep breath. Optimistic, sharp, alert. Shoulders back, chin up. He was prepared for anything right now. As confident as he felt walking out on the soccer pitch. He rested his backside on the edge of Dad's car. From his pocket, he removed a pair of sunglasses he'd found at the bottom of his clutter box and put them on. Now he felt the part, properly secret agent-like. While waiting for Roxy, he could observe Winell Road without any of its freaky residents knowing. They would just think he was relaxing in the sunshine. The lack of actual sun in the sky was an obvious defect in the plan, but the likes of Petula and George weren't going to notice those sorts of details. He also pulled from his pocket the notebook and pen from his alien card collection and, settling into as natural a pose as he could, he waited.

Petula's curtains were the first to twitch. Jack smirked. Today she wasn't the only one spying on the neighbors.

Then George appeared, placing only one foot out of his front door. His eyes darted in every direction before fixing on Jack.

Jack whistled a series of notes and drummed his fingertips on the hood of Dad's car.

After at least a minute, George, armed with his grubby, yellow watering can, shuffled out to his driveway. With occasional glances in Jack's direction, he bent down to tend his sorry-looking plants, stroking their sparse leaves and offering each a glug of water.

Next to show was the Fann family. Mrs. Fann, as usual, was first to burst out of the front door, and following in perfect formation were the mini Fanns, wearing their matching yellow t-shirts and brown pants.

Jack silently snickered. It was as if they were acting out a scene of pond life—mother duck and her ducklings.

All was peaceful over at numbers 2 and 3, the supposedly empty houses. Roxy's house was quiet this morning, too. Maybe she was sleeping in. It'd been a late night after all. Jack was grateful Mira wasn't around. What was it with her? It might be a good idea to ask Roxy a few subtle questions. He'd have to tread carefully, though, bearing in mind it was her mom. But it could be that Mira had a few issues *upstairs*, and this would explain her peculiarities. Yes, he'd ask Roxy, just as soon as she came out.

"Who are you supposed to be? James Bond?"

Jack leaped off his dad's car and turned to the voice. Roxy was leaning on the car roof, right by where he'd been sitting.

"Where did you come from?"

"I've been out for ages casing the joint. What's with the sunglasses?" She unscrewed the lid of a water bottle and took a sip.

"To make me look inconspicuous."

"Well, they're not working. I'd say they're having the opposite effect."

"Why?"

"Well, normally when you come out here you're kicking your soccer ball or riding your bike. Today, you're sitting on your dad's car, wearing a pair of sunglasses—when it isn't even sunny—and writing in a notepad. I'd say that makes you look pretty suspicious."

Maybe she had a point. Although Jack couldn't remember having ridden his bike since Roxy had arrived at Winell Road. She'd probably spotted it leaning up against the wall of his house.

Jack removed his sunglasses. "Apart from Petula, no one ever pays me the slightest bit of attention anyway. I could be running about naked and no one would bat an eyelid."

"I'd rather you didn't, thanks," Roxy said. "I've already

seen the type of underwear you wear, and that was bad enough."

Jack cringed and turned away. He'd hoped she'd forgotten about that. Fighting off a blush, he quickly changed the topic.

"Anyway, what happened to you last night? How did you get above ground? I had to shut the basement door because Dad caught me on my way back down to find you."

"Oh, I came through the basement door. Followed the arrows."

"It was probably you who disturbed Dad in the first place, then. He thought we had burglars."

Roxy snorted. "Really? Were you in trouble?"

"Nearly, but I managed to worm my way out of it."

"Why are you spying on everyone anyway?" Roxy said, hopping up onto the bonnet next to Jack.

"Well, I was thinking, they're weird, all of them. Too weird for it to be coincidence how they happen to live above an alien world. I mean, look at them; look at George and the Fanns. I think they're involved. I think they might be aliens."

"Seriously?" Roxy asked, raising her eyebrows.

"Yeah, I'm serious."

"But _you_ live here. And so do I."

"I know, I thought about that. Maybe allowing some normal people to live here stops anyone getting suspicious."

"I guess."

"But the rest of them, they're crazy weird."

"Well, in that case, we need to get inside their houses and have a look around, you know, for any secret basement door-type things."

Jack laughed. "You're a lunatic." He studied Roxy's face. Oh no, she was actually suggesting it, for real. "What planet are you from? We can't do that."

"Why not?" she asked, grinning and showing off a set of bright white teeth to match her hair.

"Roxy, not only is that breaking and entering but who knows what any one of them would do if they caught us roaming about in their house—they might never let us leave. They could tie us up and torture us, or cut off our heads and eat our brains, or—"

Roxy laughed. "You watch too many movies. I'm good at not getting caught, surprising for someone so tall, right?"

Yes, that was pretty hard to believe. "So *if* I agree, whose house do we start with?"

"Petula's. You knock on her door, and I'll hide. When she opens the door, I'll sneak in and you run off."

Before Jack could argue, Roxy was already striding over to The Die. He caught up. Was he really going along with this?

They reached Petula's front door.

Jack couldn't be sure if he'd ever seen it up this close before. It was beautiful, with incredibly minuscule and detailed markings covering every inch. Sparkling gems were embedded randomly in the black wood. Petula had obviously gone to a lot of trouble decorating it.

Jack moved his face closer to the markings. Was there a pattern to them? It was like... writing.

"Ready?" Roxy squatted beside him.

He pulled his face away from the door. He wasn't ready but knocked anyway and listened, braced, ready to run and hide.

And then it came: a creaking and a squeak and the door flew open. He dived for cover and, sprawled out on the ground, waited. A few seconds of silence then SLAM!

He peered round, Roxy had gone. Had she got inside? Jack could only lay low and wait for her return. He crouched down and leaned against the wall.

Straight ahead were numbers 2 and 3. He surveyed each of them, from their curved roofs to their red front doors.

Someone had to be living there. His whole life they'd been empty, but each roof tile was intact, no uncontrollable ivy had covered any brickwork, paintwork wasn't peeling from the front doors and the windows were clean. No. No way were they abandoned. No way.

Jack shot a look back at number 2. Something had moved. Without a single blink, he stared. What was it? A bird? A reflection in one of the windows?

And then he knew.

The blue sedan parked out the front, before, it had

faced the house, but now it was diagonal and the head-lights were pointing at him.

A chill, icy and harsh, flooded through him. It couldn't be. No one was inside the car. No engine had started. It would be impossible to turn a car around that fast. He was seeing things.

Suddenly Roxy dived on the ground beside him. Her pale skin almost glowing, her eyes sparkling.

"Awesome! You should try that some time," she said. "We can cross Petula off the list, I think. She's an odd one for sure but I don't believe she's here for anything more than a bit of spying, she—"

"We're being watched," Jack said, his eyes transfixed on the car.

Roxy lifted her water bottle to her lips. "By who?"

"The blue car parked over there." Jack nodded toward the sedan.

Roxy snorted and spat out her water. "What?" she asked, wiping her chin and rubbing her splattered white t-shirt.

"The car, it moved to face me."

"By itself?"

"Yes."

"Righto."

"It did, Roxy, I saw it." Jack fixed her stare.

"In that case, I think a visit to that very house is in order," Roxy said, waggling her eyebrows.

She sprang to her feet and handed Jack her bottle. He

held his breath in amazement as she disappeared out of sight.

And again, he sat alone, now being watched by a car. And alien neighbors. He glanced around. He couldn't see them but could feel their presence.

The forest, he could hide in the forest. Out of anyone's view.

Forcing himself to get up, he took a gutsy peek inside number 2's blue car as he passed. A regular car. Inside and out.

But it *had* moved, he was sure.

Safely inside the woods, Jack sat on a tree stump and once again waited for Roxy. He fidgeted around, trying to get comfy, but couldn't keep still. Which way should he face? In which direction could he best keep watch on Winell Road?

Jack's skin tingled. Something creepy was going on. The forest looked the same as always, but eeriness lingered there today. It had swallowed him and Roxy up yesterday, so who knew what else it was capable of or what other dangers could be lurking.

SNAP!

Jack spun around.

SNAP!

Now it came from another direction.

SNAP! SNAP!

It was happening everywhere. Something was there. Moving. Hiding.

Jack stood. What was it?

His heart stopped as a stick slid from one spot to another and then stopped. Out of the corner of his eye, he saw another stick. And then another. His eyes darted all around. The forest was teeming with them. Moving sticks that, on closer inspection, appeared to have two arms and hands clutching on to some leaves.

Were they coming for him? Were they aliens? Jack guessed both answers were likely to be yes.

A louder noise indicated something else was travelling fast in his direction. Now what? Did they have a massive stickman leader?

Poised, hands held up in a karate pose—not that he knew karate—he tried to be ready. Suddenly he spotted Roxy running towards him through the trees. She slowed to a walk as she neared and then stopped, her top half flopping forward.

"Empty," she forced out through heavy breathing.

"That's awesome, but this forest isn't," Jack replied as the sticks continued their seemingly random movements.

"What?" Roxy straightened up.

"All around us. Aliens. We need to get out of here." Jack's voice dropped to a whisper. He began backing away. Roxy copied.

"My house or yours?"

"Mine," Jack said.

"GO!"

CHAPTER FIFTEEN

THE CARDS

B oth of them bolted from the forest and out onto Winell Road.

Jack didn't care that Petula was staring or that the blue sedan was back facing the house. They ran straight across the road, through Jack's front door and up the stairs to his bedroom.

He gently closed the door and switched on his TV. Roxy slumped onto his bed and once again attempted to catch her breath.

"Why have you put that on?" she asked, her head jerking in the direction of the television.

"So we can talk without Mom and Dad hearing us. They're already suspecting something, and I can't afford to get in any trouble, not when things are getting so serious."

He walked to the other side of his bed and grabbed his backpack from the floor.

He emptied the contents of it furiously onto the bed, Roxy looking on.

"Now what are you doing?" she asked, frowning.

"It struck me, out there in the forest," Jack replied. "And down in the alien world... in that control room." Jack spread out his alien cards over his comforter.

"Okay... "

"I recognized things. Aliens. I couldn't work out why, but I knew I'd seen some of them before."

He'd found it. Triumphantly holding up one of his cards, he handed it to Roxy. As her eyes skimmed across the card, he silently read it with her.

Tronchon

Resembling earthly sticks, this alien comes from Daru. It is well camouflaged and always found in vast numbers. It fires self-produced weapons with incredible accuracy.

Strength:250

Danger:1000

Sight:50

Hearing:50

Intelligence:750

She'd hardly finished before Jack plucked another two cards from the messy pile and shoved them into her hand. Without looking up she took them and continued reading.

Quabbe

A primitive alien from planet Wawan. It is a sticky, structure-less organism without sight or hearing organs. It senses predators with

its many tongues and diffuses into the surface it is in contact with.
Strength:75
Danger:100
Sight:0
Hearing:0
Intelligence:50

And another.

Vlufli
A combative alien from planet Ala, always on the front-line of
intergalactic battles. With wolf-like features, it spins at immense
speeds and shoots burning lasers at its enemy.
Strength:135
Danger:620
Sight:60
Hearing:70
Intelligence:750

He handed her one final card. "Remember this guy?"
Roxy read.

Go'Drauht
A large threatening statue-like alien from Kolossos. Often used for
security due to its incredible fighting abilities, strength and size. It
cares for no one and nothing and only takes orders from its leader.
Best avoided.
Strength:210

Danger:900
Sight:50
Hearing:50
Intelligence:600

Roxy put the cards down and gradually stood up. "This is getting weirder."

"Tell me about it. I've had these cards for years and always thought the aliens were made up, not real."

Jack didn't know if he felt happy about his discovery. His brain was so full of information it made him dizzy. One good thing, he now knew he wasn't crazy—he *had* seen those aliens before. It didn't explain Agnes and Alan being familiar, though, that confused matters in a whole new direction.

Roxy plopped onto the bed, and Jack joined her, resting his throbbing head in his hands.

"Hey, this is a good thing, Jack," Roxy said. He looked across into her arctic eyes. She reached out and took one of his hands, steadying him.

A rush of warmth tingled over his skin.

"We've got to study these cards," she said. "Maybe the information can help prepare us for what's to come next. We need to get that Vitax and protect it with everything we've got."

She was right. Maybe this could work to their advantage. And maybe this would be the difference between life and death.

CHAPTER SIXTEEN

THE SPINNER

"This is delicious, Mrs. Mills, thank you," Roxy said, stuffing half a cheese sandwich in her mouth.

Jack grunted in agreement. His mouth was so full speech was simply not possible—unless he wanted to lose most of what he was chewing.

"You're both very welcome. It's important to have a good meal in between each adventure," Mom said, brushing some crumbs from the table and into her hand.

Jack grumbled into his next mouthful. *Adventure*. He wasn't five.

For hours, he and Roxy had studied the alien cards until the letters were just a jumble. Eventually, hunger had got the better of them and, as if she could read minds, Mom had already prepared a feast when they slumped into the kitchen with groaning bellies.

Jack looked at his mom. How could he ever have suspected her? She was odd, but normal-odd compared to what he'd seen over the past day or two.

Scarfing down a combination of a cheese-flavored

chip, half a tomato and the crust from a ham sandwich, Jack cringed as an overpowering smell accompanied the tray of cakes that his mom pulled from the oven. Uh-oh. She'd been baking.

"Here you are, Honey Surprise Buns," she announced, placing the tray in the center of the table.

"Ooo, I like honey," Roxy said, eyeing them.

Roxy wasn't aware of Mom's diabolical culinary creations. Jack, however, knew exactly what they were getting into. "What's the surprise, Mom?"

"Well... " Mom began, sitting down at the table, "...I wanted to use up some leftovers, and in the fridge I found an onion, a clove of garlic and some beef... "

"You've put cooked beef in a cake?" Jack asked. Had he heard her correctly?

"Oh no, I didn't cook it. That's the surprise... each bun has a *raw* filling."

Jack glanced at Roxy. She was dead still, her cheeks bulging like a hamster. Guilt trip. He should've warned her before she'd taken a bite. *Right, think quick.* He needed to help but without offending Mom in the process.

He spotted a box of tissues on the counter.

"Mom, could you pass me another tissue, please."

She nodded and, the moment Mom's back was turned, Jack signaled to Roxy. She spit her mouthful into the napkin on her lap. At the same time, Jack grabbed four of the buns and shoved them into his backpack.

"Mmm, not bad," Jack said, pretending to swallow as

Mom returned to her chair, a tissue in her hand.

She did a double take at the now half-filled tray of cakes. "Wow! You two did enjoy them!"

"Yes, Mrs. Mills, delicious, thank you," Roxy said, rubbing her middle in fake appreciation, yet a decidedly even paler look on her cheeks.

Jack stood, putting his backpack on his shoulder. "Thanks for the food, Mom. I think it's time we headed off." He nodded for Roxy to follow.

"Thanks again for the lunch," Roxy said, tailing Jack from the room.

"You're welcome," Mom called after them.

Out of Mom's earshot, Roxy made a choking sound. "I cannot believe I nearly ate a cake stuffed with raw meat."

"And onion and garlic! I wonder if there was actually any honey in them at all!" Jack joked.

Roxy snorted. "Don't! Hopefully that'll be our only close shave today!"

*****

"Codebreaker... check. Alien cards... check. Supplies... check."

It was last-minute preparation time in Jack's bedroom.

Today's goal was simple: get past the Go'Drauhts, go through the huge door covered in symbols, take the Vitax, then bring it back to his bedroom, and wait for the

Freogans.

Something a lot bigger than a butterfly was turning somersaults in Jack's stomach. His body was shivering despite him not feeling in the least bit cold.

"Ready?" Roxy asked, wrapping her fingers around the doorknob.

"Ready as I'll ever be," Jack replied.

A surge of importance rushed through his body. This just couldn't be happening to him; the boy with *the* dullest life on the planet and no real talents was about to embark on the Milky Way's most serious and, possibly, most deadly mission ever.

Only a few days ago he'd been dreading the summer break, and now he never wanted it to end. But when it did, when this was over and the Freogans had their Vitax, could he go back to that life? He clenched his fists. Now wasn't the time to be contemplating this. He had to stay focused, prepared for anything the alien world might throw at him.

He nodded at Roxy, and she opened the door.

Both of them squealed and jumped back... as did Mom.

She was standing on the landing, her hand formed into a fist and raised, about to knock on Jack's bedroom door.

"Goodness, Mom! What are you doing there?" Jack said. Had she been listening outside the door? Had they said anything about where they were going or what they were about to do?

"Well, it's my house!" Mom's voice was wobbly. She

straightened her cardigan, her composure clearly shaken. "I was coming to ask you if you'd mind steering clear of the basement today. Your father has a deadline to meet, and it would be much appreciated if you could let him work with no interruptions."

Of all days! They'd been banking on using the basement door to access the alien world. Now what?

"No problem, Mrs. Mills," Roxy replied.

Jack glanced at the sickly sweet smile Roxy wore. The girl must have taken acting classes.

"Thank you, Roxy."

Jack peeked around his door as Mom hurried upstairs. With a giant frown, he flopped on the bed. "Well, now what do we do?" he said, raising his palms to the heavens.

Roxy closed the door. "Why don't we try the pillars?"

"Honestly, Roxy, there's no point. I tried the Codebreaker all over and no opening appeared. There is no other way..."

But Roxy had stopped listening. She edged towards the window, staring up at the clouds. Now what was she doing? Sometimes she was as weird as her mom. Well, almost.

"What is it?" Jack asked, following her gaze up into the cloudy sky.

"There." Roxy pointed. "Don't you see it?"

Jack's eyes searched every inch of the sky. What couldn't he see? "No. What?"

"That random blob, darting about up there."

Again Jack searched, and this time he spotted it.

Yes! There it was: a dark, circular shape moving erratically in and out of the clouds. There was only one thing it could be. He pushed past Roxy to get to his telescope and whipped off the lens cap before peering through and adjusting the focus.

"It's moving closer, I think."

Jack quickly gauged exactly *how* fast it was approaching. Within seconds it was large enough for him to make out its shape.

"Oh my… Roxy, I've seen that spaceship before. It's the Spinner. I saw it down there in the alien world when we first fell through the trapdoor."

Jack looked at Roxy. She was already looking back at him. No words were necessary. She had to be thinking the same thing as him.

CHAPTER SEVENTEEN

BACK UNDERGROUND AGAIN

"Quick!" Roxy cried. "Let's get out there."

Grabbing the backpack, they rushed from the house and straight into the forest.

Sprinting as fast as was physically possible—Roxy a little faster than Jack because of her leg-length advantage—they weaved their way around trees and over ferns until Jack spotted the arched branch of the tree they'd chosen to build their fort under. Any chance of the army of Tronchons being in that part of the forest was of little concern right then.

"There!" he shouted, pointing to steer Roxy in the right direction.

As they neared the tree, Jack felt the ground begin to rumble and, looking up, he caught sight of The Spinner through the branches.

The spaceship plummeted as he stumbled on the vibrating ground. It was going to crash. Jack's jaw fell. It looked like it might. And right on top of them. The treetops slowly separated as if an invisible giant was forcing them apart with its hands, and, at the same time, the ground started opening up.

It was happening again. He and Roxy had been right. The trapdoor was an entrance for spaceships into the alien world. Only last time, the spaceship must have been invisible. It was the only explanation as to why they hadn't seen it before. But why wasn't this one invisible? Maybe the aliens flying it had tapped into his visual fields, like the Freogans had done.

Which could only mean one thing: they wanted him to see it.

Jack struggled to his feet. He threw himself at a tree trunk and clung as tightly as he could. Roxy, too, hugged one like a koala.

The Spinner whooshed down through the trapdoor.

"Now what?" Jack shouted to Roxy. Were they doing the right thing?

"We're going to have to jump," she shouted back.

What? was going to be Jack's next word, but it didn't even have a chance to form on his tongue. Roxy had already leaped into the hole.

There was no time for fear to kick in, or doubt for that matter. The trapdoor was closing up. The trees were now diagonal as the ground returned to normal.

"Here goes nothing!" Jack cried as he, too—with a hop, a skip, and a jump gigantic enough to impress any Olympic athlete—disappeared into the blackness.

The fall seemed to last forever, and for a moment, Jack wasn't actually sure if he was falling at all. Maybe the trap-door was a portal, too.

But just as thoughts of when he was going to land, and what on, cropped up, he made out the openings of several tunnels approaching below. He immediately pushed together his feet and pressed his arms tight to his sides, just in time to slip inside one. Feeling something squidgy under him, he was now sliding fast, twisting and turning, up and down, and around corners he didn't even know were coming. He was gaining speed, whizzing at a million miles per hour—at least.

Thick, wet globules splashed and splattered all over him. Bits were going in his eyes and mouth, and one went right up his nostril. Not a pleasant sensation.

Just when Jack was sure he'd be spending the rest of his life in this bizarre chute, he shot out the end of it.

Stuck for a moment in mid-air with his legs and arms flapping about, he splatted straight down into something soft. And brown. And extremely smelly. A stench Jack could hardly have forgotten.

"Not again! What is this stuff?" he said, checking out a sample of it in his palm.

Unexpectedly, a voice replied. "My first guess would be poo. Maybe alien poo." Roxy's head popped up among the slimy substance.

Jack burst into cackling laughter. "Look at you!"

Her white, wild hair now lay flat on her head, streaks

of brown running through it. Her face had lost its paleness with squidgy blotches dotted all over.

Jack snorted and grabbed his belly.

"Well, you don't exactly look like a rock star either!" Roxy said, unable to hold back her own giggles. "Let's get out of here before the whiff makes me puke."

Not ready to stop laughing, Jack wobbled an agreement. The smell was breathtakingly bad.

Wriggling and squirming, they eventually fought their way to the end of the poo pile.

Now, standing beside Roxy, Jack managed to calm himself and wipe away the laughter tears. He picked off as much brown stuff from his clothes as he could, but it wasn't easy. It seemed to have stuck like gum.

"Right," Roxy said, "we have two doorways ahead of us. Question is, do we split up, one through each door, or do we stick together?"

"Well, I don't have a coin to flip, but at the same time, I'm not sure if I want to face any aliens alone."

"That doesn't help much. I say split up."

The light-hearted moment was over. Jack considered the options for a minute. Splitting up didn't feel right.

"No, we stick together."

"If you say so. Which doorway?"

"The right one." Mom had always taught him to trust his instincts, and the right tunnel felt like the correct answer. It looked the same as the left, totally uninviting, but something was swaying him toward it.

With no time to waste, they stepped inside.

Sticking close to Roxy, Jack tried to prepare for any movement or sound that might bring danger, but the right-hand tunnel turned out to be *the* shortest of all the mysterious passages he'd ever experienced.

He tried not to show his relief to Roxy.

The tunnel had brought them to a familiar place. It was the cave where Jack had first laid eyes on The Spinner. They'd come out on the same level as where Agnes and Alan had been with the giant railway track several feet in front. And it wasn't empty.

A spaceship, slightly smaller than The Spinner, maybe closer to the size of a jumbo jet, was being examined by the multi-armed Werks.

Agnes stepped into view. Jack threw himself against the tunnel wall. Roxy stood flat against the other side. He held his breath for a moment before peering into the cave. Agnes was still there, her chubby hand holding the same clipboard. Jack looked closer. It wasn't a clipboard but more a type of computer screen, like a tablet, displaying a series of shaded gray shapes and symbols. Symbols that were like the ones on the archway and the enormous door.

More movement on the other side of the track stole Jack's attention. Two Go'Drauhts patrolled up and down, their arms once again held behind their backs.

Security must've been tightened since the last time they'd been down. That couldn't be good.

BOOM! BOOM!

Footsteps approached fast. Jack ducked into the passage again, pressing himself even flatter against the wall. Two more Go'Drauhts passed by, this time on his side of the track.

Things were getting more complicated by the second.

It was plan time. Waiting until the stomping statues sounded more distant, Jack whispered to Roxy, "What now?"

"Either we go back and try the left-hand tunnel, or we go out there." Her head jerked in the direction of the cave. "If I remember from last time, there are more doors and archways along here, so we could slip into one of them."

Jack took in her words. No, hitting the reverse button wasn't a good choice, they needed to press forward, he was adamant about that.

"Option two," Jack said. Roxy nodded.

The pair waited for the Go'Drauhts to walk by in the opposite direction, and then they crept out past Agnes. Jack afforded a quick glance up at the spaceship beyond.

It was awesome. With shimmering gold, smooth bodywork, it was shaped like an upside-down ice cream cone. Who or what got to fly something like that? It was incredible. Probably fast, too. Maybe faster than the speed of light. Or sound. Jack couldn't remember which was faster. But that didn't matter—it was bound to be amazing.

"Jack!" Roxy was beckoning him to catch up. Without realizing, he'd dropped back and was jeopardizing their cover.

Speeding up, he followed her under an archway. The rocky walls soon changed to the shiny metal variety, and they arrived in a rectangular area with six identical doors.

Jack sucked in a deep breath. "More doors! Whoever built this place seriously had a thing for doors."

He knew his attempt at humor didn't help. They needed to get back to the tunnels he'd marked with the Codebreaker's pen. That way they could get to the control room and find the Vitax. But how? Which way?

Someone was coming, humming a tune. Was it Agnes again?

With no time to talk, Roxy and Jack separated and each dived through a door.

CHAPTER EIGHTEEN

THE PHOTOS

With short sharp breaths, Jack stood peeking out of a gap in the door. It was Agnes all right. He remained concealed while she entered an opposite room.

Oh no! Was that where Roxy had hidden? He hadn't had time to see where she'd gone, but he was helpless. All he could do was watch and wait. This could be bad.

Very bad.

Several minutes passed and nothing happened. Jack decided to hold out for a bit longer and turned away from the door to investigate where he was.

The room was small and gloomy, about the size of a large elevator, but Jack was instantly struck by its décor.

The walls were plastered from floor to ceiling with pictures, or were they posters? He moved closer. Creepy, they were photographs. Photographs of people. It reminded him of a detective's office where the clues to a crime were being pieced together. There was no furniture of any kind in the room. It was empty, except for the photos.

An ice-cold sensation rushed through Jack's veins. The

people in the photos, he knew them. All of them.

There was George with his watering can, and further down the Fanns huddled together on their driveway, and off to the side one showing The Die and Petula's face pressed up to the glass of one of her windows.

And then he saw Mom and Dad.

What in the world was going on? Who had been photographing his parents?

With his fingers running across the photos, he moved quickly from one side of the room to the other, looking high and low at each and every one. There were hundreds of pictures of the residents of Winell Road.

As he reached the back wall, he let out a horrified moan. A photo of him. And one beside that of Roxy. But not just one, hundreds.

The entire back wall was a collage dedicated to the pair of them. Jack's hands trembled their way to his cheeks.

The images had been taken over the course of many years. In some he looked young, maybe six or seven, but in every photo the background was the same—Winell Road.

Goosebumps covered his skin; he stumbled backward.

Were he and his neighbors being monitored as part of some mass experiment? Researched and studied for information. If George and Petula weren't aliens themselves, then could it be that horrific procedures had already been carried out on them? Was that the reason they looked and acted so strangely? Would he and Roxy be next? Or Mom and Dad?

Jack wanted to stop looking, but he couldn't. Struggling to take in what he was seeing, one photograph caught his eye.

There he was, looking up at the sky outside his front door. It was the day of the encounter, although the spaceship wasn't visible. But that wasn't the reason this particular picture had caught his attention. It was something in the background. Moving as close as he could, his nose almost pressing against the photo, he focused on a white ball in the window of number 4. He could make out a ghostly face just below. And then it struck him.

The white ball was hair. Curly white hair.

Standing inside number 4 was Mira.

But that wasn't all. As Jack's eyes shot from photo to photo, it was now plain to see that the same pasty face, the same hair, unmistakably belonging to Mira, was in the background of every photo. Yet more disturbingly, she was there in the photos of when he was younger.

She was no new neighbor.

Mira had been watching Winell Road for many years.

CHAPTER NINETEEN

THE CAPTURE

"Aaiieee!"

The shriek ripped through the air. Jack rushed to the door and looked out as Roxy was dragged through a doorway by a hairy, black, pig-faced beast wearing a belt of weapons. Her thrashing had no effect on its clutches.

"You've got the wrong one! You've got the wrong one!" she shouted, her feet the last thing to vanish.

He needed to help her. Jack took in a deep breath and left the room of photos to follow them. He was thankful to get out of there.

The door Agnes had gone through was wide open. Jack glanced inside. There was no sign of her. Stepping past, he paused, frowning, and looked back inside. The interior—it couldn't have been more out of place.

Striped wallpaper decorated the walls of a small entrance hall, with framed hand-drawn artwork hanging up on both sides. A wooden cabinet sat on one side with a folded newspaper and a leather wallet on top, and a pair of brown suede shoes was placed neatly side by side on the maroon carpeted floor.

Jack's eyes continued along the striped wallpaper, through an archway and into another room. He could hear the crackle and pop of a fire. Tiptoeing through the door, he peered around the wall at a beige sofa in front of an open fireplace, a coffee table with two steaming mugs and a television blaring out a crescendo of music marking the tense moment of a program.

Edging forward, Jack saw someone. It looked like a boy, sitting on the squashy sofa. The back of the boy's head jerked in time with a fight scene on the screen. His creamy locks flicked up, and Jack could make out something brown hooked behind the boy's ears. A pair of glasses.

Jack knew that head, those glasses. But it couldn't be.

"Andy?"

BANG! BANG!

Jack jumped back as an enormous, metal screen slammed down in the archway. He turned to see another behind him blocking the exit back to the hallway. He was trapped in the little room with the artwork and cabinet. He could no longer see the boy on the sofa nor hear the grunts and groans of the fighting actors. The warmth of the fire had gone, replaced by a sudden chill. Jack stared around with just his pounding heart for company, and waited in the silence. What was happening?

A green fog poured in from each corner, taking just seconds to surround him.

Pulling his sleeves over his hands, he covered his nose and mouth and threw himself to the floor.

Smoke rises—he'd paid attention at school during that lesson. Only this couldn't be smoke. It seemed to be following him, forcing its way through his clothing and in through every pore.

Dizzy. Confused. His body felt numb. His mind slowed down, emptying all its thoughts and images. He was slipping away. Fighting it wasn't possible.

His head hit the ground. His eyes rolled shut. He was done for.

CHAPTER TWENTY

THE DUNGEON

So calm. So relaxed. Life was good. Amazing, in fact.
Jack smiled and stared into the blackness.

It seemed endless, open, strangely inviting. Life without limits, without restriction. Was he in heaven? No, that was silly, he hadn't died—at least he didn't think he had. Maybe he was floating in outer space. Yes, that was possible.

Jack concentrated on his body. His arms and legs felt fuzzy. He stretched his hands forward and watched his fingers wiggle in front of him. Was he controlling them? It didn't feel like it. He put his hands behind his head and continued to appreciate the nothingness.

A golden glow shot through the black sheet above. Wow! It had to be a firework whizzing by. Then there was another. And another. Had he ever seen anything so amazing? His brain didn't seem to be working; he couldn't remember a thing. Never mind, it wasn't important. Or was it?

In that second, an eerie tickle crept across Jack's skin. The firework display was great, but there was something else. A voice deep inside, trying to tell him something. What was it saying? Was there somewhere else he had to be? Nonsense, there was nowhere better than this. No time or place more important than right now, right here. Shaking the troubling feeling off, he returned his attention to the beautiful display of glittering streamers lighting up his surroundings. Maybe they were shooting stars. Or a fleet of the golden spaceships he'd seen in the cave.

He had to tell Roxy, she'd love this. But where was she? He'd seen her recently, but where? He needed to think, to delve deep and remember.

The voice returned. The image of Roxy in his mind had brought it back. He could almost hear it now. A grave feeling came with it. What? What was wrong? Roxy was in trouble, was that it?

And then it raced to the surface, screaming at him. Roxy had been captured in the underground alien world!

Jack's eyes opened. "Roxy!"

"It's okay. I'm right here."

Jack's thudding heartbeat slowed. Sitting up, his head filled with a muggy pressure. He pushed his fingertips hard into his temples.

"Where are we?" he asked, looking up at three rays of light shining through a metal grille high above them. His voice echoed, and an unpleasant smell, like sweaty feet from the school locker room, lingered nearby.

"Dungeon, I think."

Jack turned to see Roxy sitting cross-legged behind him.

He must've been sleeping. Had his head been in her lap? He touched the right side of his head. His normally spiky hair felt smooth and silky.

"Have you been stroking my hair?" he asked, frowning.

"No," Roxy snapped, shifting her position awkwardly. She folded her arms and looked away.

She had been! Huh—and she seemed embarrassed.

Roxy cleared her throat and picked at her nails. "When Agnes came along, the room I dove into was holding some kind of meeting. There was a bunch of aliens sitting around a table and making noises. I recognized some of them from your cards, but the one that seemed to be in charge was different. It looked like a giant mouth made of eyeballs, and it kept shoving flowers in. Pretty gross to be honest. Well, anyway, some hairy pig-creature grabbed me and threw me in here. What about you?"

Jack remembered the inviting lounge and the boy sitting on the couch. The boy had looked so much like Andy. Perhaps best not to say anything to Roxy. He was questioning his own sanity right now, not to mention their safety. She didn't know Andy, and besides, he was abroad with his parents, the same as every break. So whoever that boy was had been part of the trap.

"I don't know what happened to me. I hid in a room that filled with smoke." It was part truth.

What about the photos? Should he mention those? The whole mission to get the Vitax back for the Freogans seemed the least of their worries now. Neither he nor

Roxy were strangers down here, that much was evident. And how on earth could he tell her about the ghostly Mira haunting every photo? Poor Roxy. It was her mom after all. He'd need to broach that subject in a different way.

Jack stood and stretched out his aching body. His back cracked, but the mugginess in his head was clearing.

So, Roxy thought they were in a dungeon. True, it did have what he imagined to be a dungeony feel: dark and dank. He took several steps away from her and, putting his arms out in front, searched for a wall or prison bars, but instead plunged into empty darkness.

The place suddenly filled with a deep, growling groan. Something sharp pierced his face. Then his arm. Something climbed his leg. With frenzied slaps and whacks at his body, he stumbled back to Roxy and, once in the light, looked down at his body. Not a thing on him. He plonked himself down next to her and sat in a matching cross-legged position.

"Any idea what that was?" he asked, straight-backed and staring wide-eyed.

"No, but you didn't think we'd be the only ones in a dungeon, did you?"

Actually, yes, he did. And now his more-worried-than-ever mind was bursting at the seams. Whatever was hiding in the shadows was clearly something the aliens had decided was best kept in a dungeon. He moved a little closer to his companion, pressing up against her arm. Safety in numbers.

As sight wasn't a much needed sense, Jack allowed his hearing to take over. He picked up soft scurrying and the pitter-patter of tiny feet moving around, like a gang of enormous spiders circling them. They certainly weren't alone, in fact, it sounded like they were surrounded.

Jack's mind filled with giant rat-beetles planning an attack and a gruesome monster-alien preparing to devour his body. He knew he had to bring his imagination under control. Not an easy undertaking. There wasn't much to do here to take his mind off things. It's not as if eye spy was going to work, or for that matter, hide-and-seek. Perhaps talking was his best option for some temporary peace. "Where did you live before... you know, before you moved into Winell Road?"

Roxy's sullen face met his. "That's pretty out-of-the-blue."

"I'm just trying to lift the mood," Jack said. No way did he need her knowing what his brain was really up to.

"OK, well, Mom and I have lived in loads of different places lately. My dad left us about five years ago and Mom hasn't been the same since. We try out somewhere new for a few months and then off we go again."

"What's different about your mom?"

Roxy's voice and head dropped. "Everything really, she looks the same, but she used to be fun and happy. Now she's like an empty shell."

It wasn't hard to sense Roxy's sadness. Mom and Dad were misfits and often preoccupied to say the least, but loving, caring and supportive they'd undoubtedly always been. Jack had never considered life otherwise. He'd taken them for granted.

"Sorry, Roxy," he said, staring down at his shoes.

"Hey, that's okay." Her voice lifted. "You never know, maybe she's not my mom at all. Maybe she's been replaced with a zombie!"

Like a slap across the face, a whole chunk of confusion cleared from Jack's mind.

CHAPTER TWENTY ONE

THE ESCAPE

Had Roxy just found the right place for several pieces of this growing puzzle? Mira's face had been in the background of photos when he was about seven—Roxy just said her mom changed about the same time.

Maybe her last statement wasn't far from the truth. Maybe Mira wasn't really Mira but an intruder who'd been scoping out Winell Road to uncover the location of the Vitax. Far-fetched maybe, particularly as she hadn't made much progress in all these years, but could there actually be some truth to this? If so, what had it done with Roxy's real mom?

"Roxy, have you told your mom anything about here... you know, the alien world?" He leaned forward and hugged his knees, dreading the answer. "Yes" meant they were probably done for a while "no" meant they had more time.

"No, we don't really speak," Roxy replied, "but strange you ask that, because yesterday she asked me a few questions about why I'm spending so much time with you and where we go."

"And what did you say?"

"I just told her we watch TV in your bedroom and sometimes go out into the woods, why?" She looked up at him through narrowed eyes.

He'd made his enquiring too obvious. "Oh, no reason really, I just wondered," he said, avoiding eye contact.

Before her suspicions increased, Jack decided to run a few other things by her.

"Do you think it was bit of a coincidence we stumbled across the trapdoor two days after the Freogans visited me? I mean, I've lived here forever and never even seen a fox hole out there in the forest let alone a whopping great void that spaceships fly into."

"Possibly. What are you thinking—that we were meant to find it?"

"Maybe."

"You think we're being set up, don't you?"

"It's crossed my mind but it's not just that. The alien cards I've had for years, they just happen to show every alien down here. The Codebreaker just so happens to break alien codes. Don't you think it's all a bit odd?"

"So now your dad's behind it?"

"Part of me wondered that for a while, but I don't think so. If anything, I think my parents are being set up, too."

"You've lost me."

"When I hid earlier, I saw... some photos of us." Jack

glanced sideways at his new friend.

"Photos? What do you mean?"

"Photos of all of us—you know, me and you, my mom and dad, Petula. They were spread all over the walls. I think the aliens have been watching us. We're well known down here, Roxy."

Roxy stiffened. "No way! Do you think George, Petula, and the rest of them have been experimented on? OMG, do you think they're going to experiment on us?"

"That was exactly my first thought. I don't know." Jack leaned his head back against the cold hard wall.

"Do you think the aliens know about the Freogans visiting you?"

"I don't know."

"Do you think the Freogans are setting us up?"

"I don't know."

"But... but... none of this makes any sense." Roxy bit her lip, and her eyes darted from side to side.

"Tell me about it. I keep going over and over it in my mind, but I can't work out who would be doing it. And for that matter, why? All I know is we've got to get out of here and get that Vitax. Then maybe we can figure this whole thing out."

"Yeah, good plan. If there is a Vitax." Roxy stood, her hands gripped together. "Any bright ideas?"

"No, you?"

"Even if they are setting you up, can't you call your little friends to help get us out of here?"

The three Freonds! They said they'd be watching his every move, so, maybe they already knew Jack was being kept prisoner. It was a long shot, but at the moment, his only shot.

He leapt to his feet and yanked the Codebreaker from his backpack. He stared at it. How did he go about communicating via the phone with them? They hadn't actually given him any instructions. What should he do? Press some buttons, talk into it, what? Nothing seemed to work. Jack tapped his fingers impatiently on the screen. Now what?

CHINK! CHINK!

Both Jack and Roxy looked up.

There wasn't any movement above the grille, so where was the noise coming from? Jack crossed his fingers and waited.

"Friend Jack, this is not good." It was the voice of a Freogan, but no sign of which one.

"Freond, thank you," Jack said into the air above him. "Where are you? How did you get down here without being caught?" Had he summoned him?

"Up here. I've used Zapage but am still in air particle form. They will detect me soon, I don't have long. Use this key to escape."

Jack squinted into the darkness. A small object floated between two bars of the grille and dropped, landing beside Roxy's feet.

"Wicked," she said, bending down and picking up a

rusty, orange key.

"Friend Jack, you are not alone. Who is this?"

"It's okay, Freond, this is my friend, Roxy."

"No. There are *no* friends. I told you to trust no one."

"Really, we can trust her."

"No, Friend Jack, I told you to trust no one." The Freogan growled out these last words. Jack didn't like it one bit. He'd never considered what would happen if he broke their trust. What exactly were aliens capable of? He'd seen enough movies for his imagination to start kicking back in.

"Please, I'm sorry," he said. "But I think I know the identity of the other life form. I've got to get to the Vitax before it does. Where's the door this key belongs to?"

"Straight ahead, but be careful of the scavengers that are among you, once you step into the darkness, they will eat you alive."

Great! Jack's imagination hadn't been wrong. An imminent ambush was on the cards, but instead of regular giant rat-beetles, it was flesh-eating ones.

"My presence has been detected," Freond said. "But I must warn you, Friend Jack, we have heard that a map has been stolen from this world. A map showing the exact location of the Vitax. You *must* reach it first."

"Thank you and I *am* sorry."

Silence.

"So, who's the other life form then?" Roxy asked, her arms folded.

What should he say? *Your mom.* There was no way he could share his suspicions with Roxy.

"I don't *really* know," he said. "I just said it so Freond wouldn't be too cross with me."

"Right." Roxy didn't believe him, Jack knew. But escape was the only thing on his mind.

"How are we to get past these scavengers Freond mentioned? I don't want to be eaten alive. You?"

"Not today," Roxy said. "If we had some food or something, we could throw it to them. It might keep them busy long enough for us to reach the door."

Did she say food?

"Honey Surprise Buns!" they blurted out together.

"Good old Mom's baking," Jack said, foraging through his backpack.

He removed the four squashed and dented buns and handed two to Roxy. The smell of the raw beef filled his mouth even though he hadn't even tried one. He swallowed hard to remove it. "Now, the door is straight ahead. We should find it first, that way we only use the food when we have to."

"If only we had a torch to help us."

"The Codebreaker!" they chorused.

Of course! Jack held up the phone and pushed a button. A beam of light shot out, slicing through the black dungeon like a knife. Numerous thin legs dispersed into the shadows. The scavengers. He shivered, and, as he moved the light across the far wall, they continued to flee the light as more groaning filled the air.

"There!" Roxy pointed. And sure enough, Jack could make out a yellowish door thirty or so feet ahead and, halfway down it, a key hole.

"Are you ready with the key?"

"Yep."

"Ready with the buns?"

"Yep, you?"

"Yep. On the count of three, we throw and move, throw and move, got it?"

"Yep."

"Right. One. Two..." Jack took a deep breath. "Three!"

Breaking the cakes apart, they threw chunks in every direction. Furious scurrying echoed all around. It was like feeding ducks, only dangerous ones that might eat him alive. They advanced to the door, the Codebreaker's mini torch leading the way.

Jack threw the last piece of his first bun. He fumbled as he picked the second apart, he was nearly out of food. "Get the key in, Roxy, quick."

"Here, take my last bun."

As she moved to hand over the cake her arm bumped into Jack's shoulder and the food dropped to the floor.

Jack aimed the torch down to find it, but before he could make a move to pick it up, ten or so hairy, rat-sized tarantulas sped into the light and ripped the bun to pieces before vanishing back into the shadows.

"Jack! Shine the light up here!"

Immediately obeying, Jack noticed spots of blood on Roxy's arms and face. He watched her attackers scarper as the light hit them.

"I'm so sorry!" Jack cried.

He threw the final pieces of cake into the darkness as Roxy forced the key into the door and turned it. Together they pushed, and light flooded the dungeon. Jack had gotten so used to the darkness, an agonizing pain shot behind his eyes. Both of them jumped through the gap. As they slammed the door behind them, he caught a glimpse back into the dungeon. It was crammed full of aliens; not just hundreds of scavengers, but a multitude of hideous-looking creatures, great and small, all moaning and trying to clamber back into the shadows. Jack breathed out. They were lucky to be alive.

Jack looked around. They stood at one end of a short, low-ceilinged but bright room. Roxy had to duck so she didn't bang her head and as she wandered forward she reached out her fingertips to touch a brick wall at the other end.

"Dead-end. There's no way out but back into the dungeon."

"You're joking. There's no way I'm going back in there," Jack said, running a hand through his hair. He glanced back at the dungeon door—but it had disappeared. And now, in its place, stood a brick wall, identical to the one Roxy was touching.

"Roxy, look!"

She turned to see, confusion spreading across her face. "But... how?" she said.

"It's the same as..." And as Jack's gaze returned to the first brick wall, a plain, metal door appeared there instead.

"What's going on?" Roxy said.

"I dunno, but I think we'd better go through this door before things change again. As soon as we take our eyes off it, I reckon it will be replaced with something else."

Placing both palms on the cold, satiny door, Jack used every ounce of his leftover strength—and courage—and pushed. It was heavy, so he pressed his entire body weight against it. Roxy joined in.

With great effort, they managed to force open a gap large enough to squeeze through.

And then they stood, their eyes drawn to one thing.

They were at the end of a vast room that was almost empty. Situated in the center was a small silver podium topped with a glass dome. Underneath sat a rock, not dissimilar to a diamond. Every color of the rainbow and more could be seen glittering inside it.

It was dazzling. Overwhelming. Beautiful. One of the Freogans had told Jack he'd know when he found it.

The Vitax.

CHAPTER TWENTY TWO

THE VITAX

"That's it, Roxy," Jack said, his voice shaking. "We've found it."

He'd been expecting something pretty special considering it contained a power strong enough to control the galaxy, and now, standing just feet away, the Vitax was truly enchanting. He felt sure he could hear it sparkle. A smile spread across his face.

"Can you believe it?" he said.

"Yeah."

"It's amazing."

"Yeah."

"I don't think I've ever seen anything so incredible in all my life."

"Yeah."

Jack frowned up at Roxy. "Are you okay?"

She looked dumbstruck, like her eyeballs were trying to escape from their sockets, fixated on the Vitax. Not just her eyes, but her entire face seemed to have glazed over. What was wrong with her? Did this rock have some kind of magical hold over her? Jack had no idea of the extent of its powers, nor had he considered that it could be dangerous in any way—until now.

"Roxy? Are you okay?" She didn't respond.

"Roxy?" No movement.

"*Roxy!*" This time he raised his voice, making sure he spoke with force and clarity.

She snapped out of it, blinking several times and losing her balance.

"Err... what?" she said, shaking her head. "What happened?" She stumbled, totally disorientated.

"I have no idea," Jack said, "but you looked pretty freaky just then."

"That's the Vitax, Jack."

"Err, I know." Jack sighed and squatted down. "Let's get to work, what are your thoughts on booby traps?"

There was bound to be security of some description surrounding this thing, maybe sensor beams or a force field to break down. Of course, nothing was immediately obvious, but Jack had borrowed enough of Andy's action movies to know better. He needed to figure things out. They'd come this far, and not exactly trouble-free either, so he needed to stay cool, finish the job, and get back to safety in one piece—if there was such a place anymore.

Jack inspected the floor. First, they needed to get near the podium, then they could worry about lifting the lid. The floor was divided into squares about one and a half feet across, the walls and ceiling the same. It was far too clean and simple-looking. A hidden danger definitely had to be lurking.

Roxy lifted her foot to take a step forward.

"Wait!" Jack instructed, throwing his arm out to block her. "These squares on the floor, I'm gonna guess not all of them are safe. What do you think?"

Roxy shrugged. "Maybe. It would make sense, I suppose, but how are we supposed to determine which ones we can walk on?"

Jack stroked his chin. "Perhaps, if we could find something to drop on one, we could see what happens?"

"Maybe, but what if that sets off some kind of alarm?" Roxy replied.

"I don't know. But have you got any better ideas?"

"No. So what else is in your bag that we can use?" Roxy asked.

Jack dropped the backpack from his shoulders. He unzipped it and peered inside.

"How about we put an alien card on each square as a test? Between us we should be able to recall most of the details of the aliens, so no real need to keep them. Agreed?"

"If you're sure. Do you think they'll be heavy enough to set off any kind of trap?"

"There's only one way to find out."

Jack removed the first card from the pack: The Tronchon. He gingerly placed it onto the square in front of his feet. But to Jack's shock, the card dropped straight through the floor as if sinking to the bottom of a puddle of water. He stared at it, lying there like it was embedded in an enormous ice cube.

"Yes, I think they're heavy enough to set off a trap," Jack said, nodding slowly.

"Good idea of yours. I can definitely say being sucked into a floor made of sinking glass is not something I want to do."

Jack nodded again, a rather fretful one this time, and selected the next card in the pack. The Quon'kian: a moth-like alien that only lives for a week. Leaning over, he carefully tossed the card onto the next square ahead. This time it landed and remained on the surface.

"Must be a safe one. I'm going in." Jack passed his backpack to Roxy, making sure he had the remaining alien cards squeezed tightly in his hand.

He had to get this right. One small wobble or stumble and it could all be over.

Gulping, he poised himself, one foot slightly ahead of the other. Taking a deep breath, he focused and started a countdown in his head.

Three... two... one!

And he leapt... and slipped.

The floor was like an ice-skating rink. One foot touched the next square ahead. Immediately, Jack felt it being dragged down. He heaved at his ankle. No chance. The suction was fierce. He looked to Roxy.

"Take your shoe off! Quick!" she cried.

It was his only chance.

Taking care not to touch the square with any other part of his body, he yanked his foot out of his sneaker. It worked!

Wearing one sock and one shoe, Jack balanced himself on the safe square. He stared at his other shoe, now being held prisoner by the see-through floor.

"That could've been you," Roxy said behind him.

"Thanks for pointing that out."

"I'm just saying."

"Well, don't, I could be dead now."

"Sorry."

"That's okay."

"Actually, maybe that's not a bad idea."

Jack frowned. "What, me being dead?"

"No! Taking your other sneaker off, you idiot. You might grip better with bare feet."

Terrific plan. Jack removed his other shoe and his socks and launched them over to Roxy. She dodged out of their way.

"Ergh! You don't have to throw them at me," she said.

"Whoops, sorry!"

"Right, this time, don't slip, okay?"

"I'll do my best."

Jack took the next card from the pile. He'd been squeezing them so hard his palm was dented. The card showed the Vlufli. He chose a square ahead and threw. Another safe one. No second chances, he knew. This time he needed precision and balance.

Jack sprung forward and landed perfectly in the center. Closing his eyes, he privately thanked anyone, anywhere, who'd assisted him, and then turned to smile at Roxy. She replied with her own.

"Much more like it, now only ten or so to go," she said.

No time for a pat on the back. Jack looked toward the Vitax. His confidence was back. He promptly took the next alien card and, choosing another square, he threw. It remained on the surface again.

"Excellent choice."

And, like a horse in a show jumping contest, he leaped.

*****

Ten minutes later, and with only twelve cards sucked into the floor, Jack stood in front of the podium with just one tile separating them. He gazed at it, wondering exactly how many Vitax there were and if they were all as magnificent as this one. He advanced his hand towards the domed lid. A sudden angry heat surged at him. He smelled the fine hair burning on the back of his hand.

"Ouch!" He snatched his hand back to his chest and instantly the heat retreated.

Jack twisted to face Roxy. She was watching him, nibbling on her half-painted fingernails.

"There's some kind of heat field that's rushing towards me. What should I do?" he called to her, rubbing his hand.

"Can you distract it?" she suggested.

145

"Distract it?" Jack asked and, turning back, he understood her thoughts. "You mean, make it rush towards something else away from me, like a decoy."

"Yeah, then step forward when its back is turned," Roxy said.

Jack didn't feel completely sure. It could be risky, especially if whoever put the heat field there had already thought of that. But, with the clock ticking, he had to try something. He tested the idea first and flicked the next alien card over to the right and, as he did so, put his hand out in front of him. No heat. It worked.

The alien card, however, instantly caught fire, flaring up into sooty black droplets that fluttered to the ground like tiny feathers.

His heartbeat raced as he stared at the remnants.

Sinking into the floor was one thing, but being burned alive took things to a whole new level. He had only one chance at this. Lightning reactions were the key to success. Jack squeezed his eyes shut. He needed to believe in himself. He could do this.

He opened his eyes and tensed his jaw. At the same moment, he flung two more alien cards to his side and quickly stepped forward.

His jacket sleeve smoked. The heat just managed to kiss his shoulder. But he'd made it.

"Yes!" He punched the air. "So, what trap is next?" he said, turning to Roxy. But, although he could see her mouth move, all he heard was a muffled voice, as if he was underwater. It had to be the heat field preventing sound waves from travelling through. Well, something like that anyway; it sounded good. He shook his head, hoping she could at least see him clearly enough. Luckily, she seemed to understand the problem and gave him a thumbs-up. The next part was up to him.

The curved lid guarding the Vitax gave nothing away. It looked like a regular piece of well-polished glass.

Shoving the rest of the alien cards into his jeans' pocket, Jack hovered his hands inches above the glass and moved them over it like a fortune teller. Nothing indicated a trap of any kind. He took a card from his pocket, touched the glass with one of its corners, and waited for a reaction. Nothing happened. He repeated this a couple more times, but things remained the same.

Putting the card back into his pocket, he rubbed his hands together and touched the lid. With gentle manipulation, he discovered that it flipped open like a bin lid and now, with it exposed to the world, his opportunity to take the Vitax had arrived. With just his fingertips, he warily lifted it from the stand and braced himself for a rush of powerful energy through his body.

Disappointingly, no such feeling arrived. Instead the Vitax felt like any old rock from his backyard, rough and jagged. Its sparkling had subsided, and its brilliance was not so obvious. But Jack clasped it; there wasn't time to worry about that now. He had to return to Roxy and get the heck out of there.

Turning to face her, almost every hair on Jack's body stood at attention. Something was there, in the room with them. He glanced around—he may not be able to see it, but he could feel it.

With his sixth sense now on high alert, Jack moved with some haste.

Removing another card from his pocket, he repeated the action to fool the heat field. But this time the card didn't catch fire, it simply fell to the floor. As Jack bent down to pick it up, he felt no searing heat. The protective field had gone.

And the twelve alien cards that had previously sunk into the floor were now sitting on the surface, along with his shoe. The booby traps had reversed.

"Something's going on," he said, racing back to Roxy.

She didn't appear to have heard him and instead gawped at the Vitax in his hand.

"Pass it to me," she said, holding out an expectant hand.

Jack ignored her. "We need to get out of here before we're captured again."

He took his backpack from Roxy and put the Vitax inside, removing the Codebreaker as he did so. Preparation was essential if their return above ground was to go smoothly. He sat down and put his socks and shoes back on.

"Shall I hold your bag for you?" Roxy asked.

Securing the pack on his back, Jack frowned and shook

his head. "No. Let's go."

But as he turned to leave via the same door through which they'd entered, all that stood in its place were more glassy squares, as if a door had never been there.

"Oh no! It's happening again. How are we going to get out of here?" Jack exclaimed, yanking at his hair. They'd come too far now. To be recaptured was out of the question. They had to find another way out.

While the dread of defeat filled his body, a movement high up on the ceiling distracted him. It was the outline of something darting back and forth. As he focused harder, he noticed there was more than one, perhaps three in total.

"Spodians," Roxy whispered in his ear. "Remember? One of your alien cards showed an alien from Iba that camouflages into its background. A Spodian."

The memory came flooding back. "Yes! And it travels through all known substances, along with whatever touches it. Roxy! There's our escape."

"But first we need to attract them over so we can get close enough to touch one."

"Yes, yes! We need to find their weakness. Think, what else did it say about them?"

"I remember they scored really low on sight. Maybe if we stand dead still they might not see us and come closer."

"It's worth a try."

And so they froze, as if playing musical statues, but with no dancing, and this time their lives depended on winning. Sure enough, the longer they stood still, the closer the flying outlines came, until Jack felt the breeze one created as it raced past.

Next time.

And, as one flew by, he reached out and grabbed it.

Surprisingly, it was soft and fluffy, like a pair of just-washed soccer socks. His feet lifted off the ground and, looking down, he grinned as Roxy grabbed on to her own Spodian.

He soared higher, up towards the ceiling, and then Jack's invisible ride hit the accelerator. Straight towards the wall.

"This had better work!" Jack said, squeezing his eyes shut and awaiting the whack—but it never came. Instead, he became aware of a murmuring buzz. Opening his eyes, he was now sailing high above the control room. Hundreds of aliens hurtled about below. He managed a glance behind. Thankfully, Roxy was following.

The Spodian now circled the room. Jack had to maneuver his body to avoid hitting the transporting tubes, but it didn't take long until he felt dizzy. He had to get back on his feet. The archway they'd stood under the first time they discovered this place was visible. Once there, they could follow the Codebreaker's marks on the passageway walls and get back to the basement door. This was it! The home straight. All he needed to do was let go. Easier said than done when whizzing about thirty feet in the air. But, without warning, the Spodian took a sudden nose dive towards the ground. With no time to think, Jack took the opportunity and released his grip. He rolled gymnastically to a stop.

He scrambled to his feet, now surrounded by a lot of startled aliens. Well, he assumed they were startled, only it was hard to tell exactly, seeing as some of them didn't appear to have faces.

A commotion elsewhere in the room switched the focus of the aliens away from Jack. Was it Roxy?

As he rushed over, she lay slumped on the floor, an agonized expression on her face and, as he got nearer, he understood why.

She must've hit something sharp when she fell from the Spodian. Her leg was deeply cut, blood pouring from the gaping wound. Incredibly, she was managing to climb to her feet when he reached her.

"Roxy! Are you okay?" Jack cried, grabbing her arm to provide her with any support he could.

"Yeah, yeah, I'm good. Let's go."

And, hand in hand, they stood facing the archway. And a path laden with aliens.

Out of the corners of his eyes, Jack saw several Go'Drauhts approaching in the wings. If he and Roxy ran, they could reach the archway before them. So, tightening his grip on Roxy's hand, he sprinted, heaving her along with him. They ran past the aliens, under the archway and into the metal passages. Jack switched the Codebreaker's light on and, leading a limping Roxy, he shone it at the metal walls to reveal the tiny blue arrows directing them home.

With the Go'Drauhts closing in on them, he used every ounce of his remaining energy until they veered around the final bend.

There it was—the basement door.

With all their might, they threw their bodies against the door and furiously wiggled the handle. For the second time in their lives, it opened just in time as stomping footsteps rounded the corner behind them.

Slamming the door shut, they collapsed onto the cold basement floor, trying to catch their breath. They'd made it. With the Vitax now safely protected in Jack's backpack, it was over. For a time anyway.

"WHAT ON EARTH ARE YOU DOING?"

Dad was standing by his desk. His eyes sat wide in his bright red face.

"Your mother told you not to come down here today, and you have deliberately disobeyed her. I have a good mind to... Roxy! You're bleeding! Quickly, up to the kitchen."

Glancing at one another, Jack helped Roxy to her feet, and they followed Dad upstairs and into the kitchen. A strong odor of coffee welcomed them and there, at the farmhouse table, sat Mom—and Mira.

"OH MY GOODNESS!" Mom cried. She jumped up from her chair and wet a tea towel in the sink. "Sit down, Roxy, you're bleeding." She gently pushed Roxy onto her chair and folded the towel to put on her leg.

Just before she did, Jack noticed that Roxy's wound appeared a lot smaller now, almost as if it had shrunk. He quickly brushed his observation aside. It had been a manic moment, and obviously the cut had looked worse at the time. His attention turned to Mira.

She sat at his kitchen table, head lowered and emotionless eyes staring at the floor, apparently not bothered in the slightest that her supposed daughter was injured. She'd probably been interrogating his poor mother for information. Jack's hands formed into tight fists. How dare this thing endanger the lives of his parents, his poor innocent parents? If only he knew its weaknesses, he'd fight it there and then.

"What has been going on with you two?" Mom's voice interrupted his rage. "This is to stop right now. Poor Roxy and Mira have just moved here, and in three days you have..." Her face suddenly screwed up. "What's that smell?"

Leaning forwards, she sniffed at Roxy, and looking over in Jack's direction, Mom stared him up and down, pinching her nose. "Have you been rolling in manure? You absolutely stink."

Alien poo. He'd gotten so used to the smell.

Jack looked over at Roxy and then down at his clothes. They were both covered in crusty brown lumps, sweat dripping from their heads. No wonder Mom was so cross.

"Mira, I am so, so sorry for my son's behavior. I am

dreadfully disappointed in him. Goodness knows what you think of us, leading Roxy into all this trouble and getting her injured like this. Let me see, my love." Mom leaned forward to remove the tea towel, but Roxy wouldn't let go of it. She pressed it harder into her calf muscle.

"It's fine, really, thanks," Roxy said. "I'm sorry for the smell, Mrs. Mills. Maybe we should get going, Mom, I could use a shower." Tying the towel tightly around her leg, she stood up.

Mira also stood and as she did dropped a large piece of half-rolled-up paper into her cardigan pocket. Jack stared at it. His body weakened as the two females passed him and left the kitchen.

A MAP!

Hearing the front door close, Jack stood alone with his parents. He braced himself for a lecturing from Mom, but it was Dad who spoke next in a frighteningly calm voice.

"Go to your room, son. Take a shower and go straight to bed. I don't want to see you for a while." He turned his head away.

Jack opened his mouth to apologize but, on looking at his parents' faces, decided it would be best to just do as he was told. He skulked up to his bedroom and, closing the door behind him, took off his backpack and removed the Vitax. Dropping back onto his bed, he studied it.

Mom and Dad were so ashamed of him, but if they only knew. If only they had an inkling of the importance of what he'd been doing, then he was sure they'd understand. But he knew deep down it was too dangerous to involve them. He had the Vitax. Now all he needed to do was wait for the Freogans to come and take it.

Jack sighed. If only it was that simple. He may have succeeded in this task, but there was no point in feeling comfortable. He'd seen those photos. Something much more serious than a stolen object was taking place on Winell Road.

What should he do next? How could he make Mom and Dad understand? How could he get them away from Winell Road before it was too late? Before they all became victims of some terrible alien experiment. Maybe it was already too late. Had he been taken underground in the past without knowing? Was that how he recognized Agnes and Alan?

But it still didn't explain the alien cards. Come to think of it, not one of his school friends collected the same cards, so how had Dad come by them? Where had he bought them?

And then there was Mira.

She wasn't new to the road; the photos were proof of that. And he'd seen a map in her pocket. Was it just a coincidence that Freond had told him of a stolen map? There wasn't one doubt in Jack's mind as to the answer.

But wait! Now she had the map, she'd be heading for the Vitax and would soon discover it missing from its plotted location. And if Jack failed to contact the Freogans in time, would Mira track it to him?

And Roxy. If all this was true, then she was in serious danger. What she thought was her mother was a dangerous alien after only one thing.

He needed to get to her, to rescue her from harm. But how?

CHAPTER TWENTY THREE

THE OTHER LIFE FORM

4:20 P.M.

Daylight crept in around the edges of the curtains. Jack had paced his bedroom, up and down, for over an hour. The Vitax never left his hand.

He'd hardly slept. He didn't dare. Just in case he missed the Freogans. But still they hadn't showed. Even fiddling with the Codebreaker didn't seem to summon them this time. No other aliens had come looking for him, either. And as for Mira—so far there'd been no sign.

His mind raced with new plan after new plan, and one after the other he'd dismissed them. All of them were riddled with flaws and destined to end in disaster. There was no way he could leave his room and face his parents. He hadn't heard them come to bed last night, and if they caught him wandering about at this time of the morning, after their reactions yesterday, they'd flip.

Jack's stomach twisted, like a fisherman had been using it to practice tying knots; like he was about to take a match-deciding penalty. He just didn't know what to do.

He felt so alone. No one to trust. No one to call for

help. This hadn't been part of the deal. How had he got caught up in this whole mess? At one point, he'd actually buzzed inside. Like he was meant to be doing this. But not now. He'd discovered things about Winell Road that meant there was no going back. Ever.

He curled up in a ball on the end of his bed and gazed at the rock in his hand. It had been so captivating when he'd first laid eyes on it yesterday, but now it was so plain, so ordinary. It had crossed his mind that maybe it wasn't the Vitax in his hand, but something completely different. It was possible that he and Roxy had made a terrible mistake, and the real Vitax was still down there, in the alien world. If this was true, then Mira would definitely have found it by now.

His mind was in turmoil. Being cooped up in his bedroom was driving him insane. He had to get out. But where was safe? Should he get on his bike and take the Vitax far away? No, he couldn't turn his back on Roxy, not if she was in danger. Nor could he abandon his parents and leave them to be experimented on by a bunch of extra- terrestrials.

One thing was for sure, moping about in his bedroom wasn't helping anyone. He was wasting time.

After putting on his sneakers, he thrust the rock into his jacket pocket, picked up the Codebreaker and, as quietly as he could, opened his bedroom door. Listening for anything that may pinpoint Mom and Dad, he tiptoed onto the landing. It was eerily silent. They were probably sleeping.

He crept down the stairs and, drawing near to the kitchen, he moved ever more cautiously. Poking his head around the door, he was in the clear. Mom wasn't there, and he couldn't see her anywhere outside. He moved down the steps, into the basement and, again, not a single sound or movement was to be found.

Suddenly, Jack's knotted stomach tightened painfully. He couldn't breathe.

The door... the basement door to the alien world was open. Wide open. Had the aliens found their way in? Or had Mira used it to access below ground? He had to get Roxy.

Jack sprinted out of his front door and straight over to Roxy's house.

The front door was ajar. Jack stood by it, listening hard for any noise within and, with just his index finger, gently pushed.

He moved inside, into the hallway.

It smelt musty, as if no fresh air had entered the house for weeks, and he could see dust suspended in the air.

The ground floor appeared to have the same layout as his house. He could see the kitchen ahead and a back door leading out to an overgrown yard framed by trees. Jack approached the basement staircase. Each step he took made his heart pound harder.

What was he doing? Surely Roxy would be in her bedroom. But something was drawing him down. Was there a

door there, too? A door into the alien world? Their basement was nothing like Dad's workshop, with its endless
piles of papers and boxes. It was empty and cold. The
reddish brickwork of the walls was visible along with the
hard, concrete floor.

Jack looked to the end of the room—there was no
door.

A huge, wooden chest lay open in the middle of the
basement floor. The same one he'd seen Mira and Roxy
carry into their house when they moved in, when he'd
first noticed Mira's odd movements. Why hadn't he tak-
en Mom's advice and trusted these first suspicions? He
could've spent more time investigating Mira instead of
leaving it until now, when things could turn nasty.

Up close, Jack could see how huge the chest actually
was. Why would anyone need a piece of furniture this big?
What did Mira and Roxy store in it? After all, it was as big
as a ... a coffin.

Jack's heart stopped beating.

He crept forwards and, as the contents became clear,
his legs buckled. His hands slapped, one on top of the
other, over his mouth. Tears streaked down his cheeks.
He shook.

It couldn't be.

No. It wasn't.

It was.

Inside lay a body, but dead or alive, Jack couldn't tell.
Its knees were bent up and head forced to one side by the

top of its prison. Its hands and feet were tied with rope and its mouth hidden by thick silver tape. On its head sat curly, white hair, now so familiar to him his first thought was that it was Roxy, but the face belonged to someone older, and there was only one person it could be. Was he looking at the real Mira?

Whispered words began echoing around him.

"You will not stop me, Jack. You will not stop me, Jack."

Over and over, the same sinister sentence.

Jack twisted around. Who was it? Where were they hiding? But he was completely alone, except for Mira's motionless body in the chest.

"You will not stop me, Jack."

He felt dizzy. The room was spinning, the walls caving in on him. He needed air.

The voice was getting louder; he could hear laughter in its tone. An evil, triumphant laughter.

"You will not stop me, Jack."

"NO!" Jack screamed and bounded from the basement and the house.

Gasping for oxygen, he crashed into a puddle and welcomed refreshing raindrops on his face.

And then it hit him.

Those words—*you will not stop me, Jack*—the fake Mira had been mouthing this to him, over and over, when she'd stared through his kitchen window on that very first day. She'd known about him then, before he'd even been visited by the Freogans. Before he'd even known about the missing Vitax. But… but how?

The photo underground. She'd been there when the Freogans' spaceship had visited him.

Bleep!

The noise broke his thoughts.

Sitting up slowly, he wiped the rain and tears from his eyes and looked at the Codebreaker in his hand. The screen was flashing. It had to be Freond-the-Red contacting him to say he was coming for the Vitax. Or maybe they'd discovered the other life form to be Mira. But it was too late. He had to let them know she'd been on to them from the start.

He pressed the display button on the phone.

A face appeared. He'd been right; they were warning him of the intruder's identity. But the face displayed was not Mira.

It was Roxy.

CHAPTER TWENTY FOUR

THE END

Mom and Dad sat huddled together in the corner of his bedroom. And there, standing beside his bed with his backpack in her hand, was Roxy. It was obvious she'd been awaiting his arrival. She narrowed her eyes and smiled at him standing in the doorway.

"I wondered how long it would take you," she said. Her voice was calm as usual, but today it was ugly. She'd been lying to him, using him to get what she wanted. How had he not seen this?

"Now I know why you were acting so strangely when I had the Vitax yesterday." Jack tried to keep his voice from shaking and giving away his fear.

"I'm surprised it took you so long to figure out," Roxy replied. "You worked out my mom was involved, though, so I suppose some congratulations are in order."

From behind the door stepped the counterfeit Mira. Jack felt more intimidated than ever. In her hand was a weapon. It looked like one of his water guns but he knew the damage it could cause would surely be horrifying.

"But, Roxy, this isn't your mom. I've just seen your real

mom in that wooden chest in your basement."

"What are you talking about?" Roxy yelled.

"A fabrication." The intruder spoke before Jack could continue. "I am your mother."

Jack glanced at his parents.

They were petrified. He could see it in their eyes. He'd never seen them look so delicate, so fragile. How could he ever have suspected them? He needed them out of harm's way, and then he could finish this.

"Please, my parents have nothing to do with this. Let them go," he said.

"Hand over that rock, and we will let you all go," Roxy replied.

"Roxy, why are you doing this?" Jack needed to understand what was going on with her.

He looked at Mira, into eyes dark and set deep into its face. He'd never really seen them properly. He stared hard. They flashed. What was that?

One of his cards had detailed an alien with eyes that did this but... what else had it said? Darn, he couldn't recall.

"Ignore him. Now, Roxy, we need that Vitax." It was the same chilling voice that had spoken to him in their basement. He turned to Roxy.

"Yes, Jack. Hand it over. Let's not make this harder than it needs to be." Roxy stepped towards him, her hand outstretched, waiting for his surrender.

"Please, Roxy... I..."

Mira lifted her weapon and pointed it at his parents. "You heard her. Hand it over."

There was nothing he could do. He was helpless. Where were the Freogans? They'd said they were watching his every move. Had they been captured? Reaching into his pocket, he removed the Vitax and handed it reluctantly to Roxy. She snatched it and spun around to face the alien she still thought was her mom.

"I have it," she said.

"And now you will hand it to me." Mira aimed the weapon at Roxy.

"But, Mom, what are you doing?" Roxy's proud expression had turned to one of horror. Jack could see Mira's betrayal was more of a shock to Roxy than to him. He stared at the alien and again, this time, he clearly saw its eyes flash red.

He remembered! The gray-edged card he'd found in his pack of alien cards.

The Axeinos—It has no true form, but takes the shape of other creatures to capture its prey. Can be identified by an occasional flash of its bright red eyes. An expert at mind control.

He needed to protect Roxy. She was innocent. As the Axeinos lifted its weapon and took aim, Jack leapt in front of the terrified girl.

BANG!

He heard it fire and felt an impact that sent him crashing to the ground.

As unconsciousness swept over him, the frightened faces of Roxy and his parents rushed towards him and slowly faded away.

CHAPTER TWENTY FIVE

THE TRUTH

J ack opened his eyes and blinked away the blurriness. The first things he saw were his mom and dad, both smiling.

Details of what happened in his bedroom were returning, but only piece by piece. Mom and Dad were okay, though. This could only be good.

Mom held one of his hands in both of hers and rubbed it with her thumbs.

"Hey, son." Dad reached forward and ruffled Jack's hair, something he'd done every day of his life—that Jack could remember anyway—but today, right now, it was the best feeling ever.

"Hey," Jack croaked, his throat sore and dry.

"Here, have a drink." Mom released his hand and passed him a glass of water. Placing her hand behind his head, she lifted him forward so he could drink. The liquid slid down his throat, instantly soothing.

"Thanks," Jack said, a little more easily. Mom lowered his head back onto the soft pillow.

He was lying in a strange bed. The room was mainly

red, black, and gray, the walls covered in stripy wallpaper, and a matching comforter was draped over him. It had to be the bedroom of someone young. There were posters on the walls of Transformers. Several shelves were filled with models of spaceships and a mini solar system that he guessed the owner had made.

There were no windows anywhere in the room, just a single door on the opposite wall.

"Where am I?" he asked, turning back to his mother.

Mom blatantly ignored his question. "How are you feeling, love?" she asked, stroking his forehead.

"Tired, but okay, I think."

"That's great."

Jack caught the weird look Mom gave Dad. They were keeping something from him.

"What's up?" he asked, but before they had a chance to answer, the bedroom door flung open.

All the energy left in his body drained away; his face tingled and his voice wedged in his throat.

A huge stone face. Golden slits for eyes. Arms behind its back. A Go'Drauht.

"No! No! Mom! Dad! Get out of here, it's dangerous!" Kicking off the blankets, Jack tried to find the strength to jump out of the bed, but weakness took hold. He felt Dad's hands grab him before he collapsed.

"It's okay, son. It's okay."

"But, Dad, they're here for me. You and Mom have to get out. I never meant for you to get hurt."

Jack's arms and legs flapped and kicked, but Dad's grip was tight and firm. No matter how much he wrestled for freedom, he wasn't going anywhere.

"Jack." Dad spoke sternly.

Jack stopped, defeated, and stared at his dad's calm face. "What's going on?" he asked, sitting back on the bed.

"Jack, there's something your mother and I need to tell you," Dad said.

Jack looked to his mother for an answer. "Mom?"

"First of all, Jack, we would like for you to meet some people." As Mom spoke, she turned to the open door and nodded to the Go'Drauht.

Jack glanced at the doorway as a procession of familiar creatures entered the room. First came Roxy and two Miras, who were followed by George, the Fann family, and finally Petula Penula.

"You recognize these people?" Mom asked.

Jack nodded, his heart banging against his ribs.

"And how about these three?" The Freogans hovered into the room.

Sitting forward, Jack stared at the peculiar row of individuals lined up at the end of the bed.

"All of us standing before you now, and every other alien you have encountered this past week, are part of the Secret Organization for Universe Protection, or S.O.U.P. as we call it. The Mills family has worked here for generations in cooperation with aliens from all of our galaxy's inhabited planets. Your grandparents, great-grandparents, and so on, and now us. We work to maintain peace and order in our galaxy and ensure other galaxies respect us and all that we stand for," Dad explained.

Jack fixed his dad's stare. "You know about the alien world? But... but... I don't understand. Dad, you're an inventor and Mom, you... you bake and grow flowers. You can't be involved, it's not possible." His own voice sounded distant.

"I *am* an inventor, Jack, but I invent tools, weapons and machinery for S.O.U.P. There is no exercise bike vacuum cleaner—although I do believe that is a darn good idea. The Codebreaker and your alien cards, I made them for you."

"That's right, and, although I do grow flowers for important reasons, I'm an expert in mind reading and alien communication. Your father accesses S.O.U.P. through the basement, and I do via my greenhouse." Mom nodded enthusiastically. "Have you ever wondered why I seem to vanish every time I go in there?"

Jack had always thought his mother hid well in the greenhouse, but now he knew she wasn't in there at all.

He couldn't speak. A million questions flooded his brain.

"Let me introduce you properly." Dad stood and made his way over to the line of people standing before Jack.

"This is Roxy, Mira and Mena. They are Keu'Panacas from Scimerian."

They approached Jack and took turns shaking his hand.

So there *had* been two Miras.

As Roxy approached, Jack glanced down at her leg. "Your cut's miraculously healed, just like your head did that first day you bashed it on a rock. I should've guessed you were an alien." It hadn't registered at the time, but now Jack wondered why he'd never questioned the disappearance of the blood that had stained her hair, or how she'd made it back to the basement door that time by following arrows invisible without the Codebreaker.

Roxy nodded then nibbled a fingernail. "Keu'Panacas can heal themselves in minutes. Sorry, Jack."

One of the Miras stepped forward. "Jack, it is such a pleasure to finally meet you properly, an absolute honor. This is Mena"—she pointed to the other Mira—"who you saw curled up in the wooden chest. I'm not really an Axeinos, I used flashing contact lenses your dad invented to make you think I was one. Clever human your dad!"

Jack was sure she bowed as she stepped away—perhaps a little over the top.

Mom continued with the introductions.

"You've met the Freogans." Freond-the-Red clasped both of its hands around Jack's, making them look pathetically small. "It is an honor, Friend Jack."

"This is George, a Keu'Plachu also from Scimerian." George also appeared to bow but in a more nervous style than the others.

Jack now understood why George ran inside his house so often; Keu'Plachus could hear noises far away and

171

would then flee from any danger. George didn't need the toilet so frequently after all.

"And the Fann family. They are Anetii from Zodzin." One by one, the mini Fanns followed Mrs. Fann to Jack's side, jabbering in their bizarre language, then toddled away.

Finally, Petula approached. With her big electric blue eyes now poking out further than Jack had ever seen, she bowed her head in a greeting.

"It's so good to meet you properly." Her voice sounded like it had come straight from a cartoon alien—electronic and multi-pitched.

"Where are you from?" Jack asked.

"Earth, I'm human just like you."

"Oh." It was all Jack could manage. Of them all, Petula looked and sounded more alien than any. She returned to her place in the line.

Jack's focus quickly switched back to the bedroom door. New visitors arrived. In walked Agnes and Alan, followed by his best friend, Andy.

"Jack!" Andy rushed to Jack's side and threw his arms around his neck. Hugging him tightly, Jack groaned, his chest still sore.

"Sorry, dude! But it's so good I no longer have to lie to you."

"Wait… What? You work for S.O.U.P., too?"

"Yes, that's why I've never been able to talk about my mom and dad. I believe you've already met Agnes and

Alan Aldred."

"You *were* the boy on the couch."

Andy nodded, smiling broadly.

Looking at the three of them together, Jack now understood why he'd found Agnes and Alan so familiar. They were like three blonde, chubby peas in a pod.

"I've been keeping watch over you at school," Andy said, the pride clear in his voice.

It made sense; he and Andy were so different, why else would they have made friends?

"At least now I know why you're so much smarter than the rest of the kids in the class. Is this your bedroom?" Jack asked.

"Yeah, do you like it? Best part of it is we're neighbors, Jack. Right now you're underground, in my house, number 1 Winell Road."

Two mysteries solved in one. There *was* a number 1 after all, and Jack had discovered exactly where Andy went for every summer break—underground.

"There's one more alien you must meet: our leader." Mom gestured to the door.

Everyone in the room stood tall and looked to the doorway. Jack did, too. He grimaced as a squelching, burping alien appeared. It resembled a mouth with eyes dotted all over the lips.

Jack remembered Roxy describing this alien before. It was scarlet and had one thick leg with five or six hand-like feet moving it along. He tried to force his face into a calm expression, but he wasn't sure if he'd succeeded, particularly when the lips parted and a loud gurgling and gargling sound erupted from within.

"This is Mrs. Atkins," Mom said. "She isn't able to speak as we humans do, but she says she is so pleased to finally be able to meet you and she welcomes you to S.O.U.P."

So *this* was Mrs. Atkins, and she was the leader of S.O.U.P. who really did eat his mother's flowers. And looking like that, no wonder she didn't leave her house.

"Mrs. Atkins is the only one left of her species. No one can say exactly how old she is, but it's billions of years," Freond-the-Red explained.

"Wow." Jack closed his eyes and fell back onto the pillow. He placed an arm over his eyes. This was all so overwhelming. His mind churned. Mom asked everyone to leave and once the door clicked shut, he opened his eyes.

"You okay?" Dad asked.

"You. It was you who set me up," Jack whispered, staring up at the ceiling. So many questions. It was all such a jumble. Where should he start? "Why? Why did you keep this from me? For twelve whole years you've been watching me living some sort of lie. I don't get it."

Dad let out a long sigh. He leaned back in his chair and looked over at Mom. She nodded.

"Jack, seventeen years ago, your mother gave birth to a baby boy," Dad said.

"But I'm twelve, what are you talking about?" Were

they now trying to tell him he was really seventeen?

"Not you, Jack, your brother, Toby."

Jack's jaw locked. He couldn't have heard that right?

"Toby Bill Mills, our firstborn, was only with us a month, Jack, before he was taken. Straight out of your mother's arms."

Jack stared at Mom. She wiped a tear from her eye with a shaking hand.

"But why?" he asked.

"It was a treacherous time, back then. A wicked gang of aliens from another galaxy was terrorizing the Milky Way. We think an insider here in S.O.U.P. leaked information to them about the whereabouts of our headquarters, and then they came... Many S.O.U.P. agents lost their lives. Several Vitax were taken. And so was Toby." Dad lowered his head.

"Is he still alive—my brother?"

"We don't know, Jack. We keep his stuff in the attic. We've never stopped searching. Even to this day, members of S.O.U.P. patrol our universe looking for him," Dad said.

"It's too painful for us to consider anything different," Mom said, "so we created Winell Road when I was expecting you, to keep you safe."

"Everyone who lives here, above and below ground, has been keeping you safe. We don't know why they took Toby but, my word, we weren't going to lose you to them as well," Dad said through gritted teeth.

Jack stared at the stripes on the comforter, unable to find any words to use. He had a brother.

"We know we should've told you about our real lives before, when you were younger, but we were so frightened of losing you, we just couldn't bring ourselves to involve you, endanger you," Mom said, another tear trickling down her cheek.

"So why now? What's changed?" Jack asked.

"That spaceship, Jack, the one that you saw outside the house..." Mom began.

"But you said you hadn't seen it." Jack frowned at her.

"We all saw it. We think that was them, the same gang that took Toby. Only this time, here to take you."

Jack's breath sucked from his body. He'd assumed that had been the Freogans' spaceship. "H... h... how come I got away?"

"We managed to surround you with a protective field strong enough to deny them your physical form."

"But how did it get to me? How did they find me?"

"We don't know. We don't know how it got past our sensors or indeed our patrols. We're investigating another mole."

"But..."

"Since Toby was taken, things have been quiet, until these past few weeks. We recognized the same strange occurrences in our solar system. It must be them, the same gang. Gaining strength, stealing protectors. But they came for you. You, like Toby, are their target," Dad said.

"Listen, Jack, we don't expect you to say anything right now, we don't expect you to understand but, please, don't hate us. We always felt like we were doing the right thing, but now it's all become dangerous again and we need you to be prepared. Why they want you, we don't know, but they will return," Mom said, yanking on the sleeves of her pink cardigan.

Jack shook. He, a twelve-year-old boy, was the target of a dangerous gang of aliens.

"Jack? Are you okay?"

"Why didn't you just tell me?" Jack's voice came out barely a whisper. "Why did you go to all the trouble setting up this elaborate prank over the past few days? I would've understood. I feel like such a fool."

"It wasn't a prank, Jack. This is a dangerous world to be part of. Not just anyone can handle what's out there. S.O.U.P. agents have to undergo training before taking a simulated test, similar to what you've just completed. We don't have much time to train you, Jack, so we decided to throw you straight in," Dad said, raising his eyebrows and nodding.

"But making all that stuff up about the Vitax…"

"No, the Vitax are real. The rock you retrieved was real, Jack, a real protector of our galaxy."

"We realize you may have been a bit scared but—" Mom said.

"A bit scared? You're kidding, right? You threw me in a dungeon with a bunch of aliens and shot me in the chest and gassed me in a cloud of green smoke and—"

"It was only an air bullet that hit your chest yesterday. And that smoke was a small dose of memory gas—a substance we use to wipe aliens' memories. We would never hurt you," Dad desperately explained.

"And the dungeon full of dangerous aliens?"

"That was real, but Roxy was with you, she'd never have let anything hurt you," Mom said.

"Please, Jack, take some time now to think it through before you judge us. We knew you'd work it out in the end, and we know you'll make one of the best alien agents S.O.U.P. has to offer," Dad said.

Jack turned away from his father and closed his eyes again. His Dad ruffled his hair, and Mom patted his shoulder before the door clicked shut. He pulled the comforter over his head and cried.

CHAPTER TWENTY SIX

THE NEW BEGINNING

Whichen Jack finally awoke, he was reluctant to leave behind his wonderful dream of flying the golden spaceship. He was safe there. Happy. He opened his eyes and discovered he was still in Andy's room. And it was Andy's face that first greeted him.

"Hey, bud. You *were* tired!" Andy looked at his massive wristwatch. "That's almost thirty-six hours you've slept for. How are you feeling?"

Jack pulled himself up to a sitting position and rubbed the sleep from his eyes. "Okay, thanks."

"I guess you had to take in a shed load of info before. How do you feel about everything?" Andy passed him a glass of orange juice.

Jack gulped it down and handed back the glass. "Thanks. Um... weird. I don't really know how to feel about it to be honest." Jack looked down at his hands. Such ordinary hands. But ordinary hands that no longer belonged to an ordinary boy. "Dang, Andy, I'm a target. Nothing is ever going to be the same again."

"You're right there, but that's a good thing. Now you're

part of us, of S.O.U.P." Andy smiled encouragingly.

Jack still wasn't sure. "But Andy, I was nearly snatched by those aliens, like my brother. They're going to come back, and I don't even know what I've done. Why Toby? Why me? Why not you?"

"Answers S.O.U.P. doesn't have."

"And why didn't they just tell me? Your mom and dad told you. I feel so silly. You were all in on it, laughing at me as I tried to solve the pretend mystery."

"It wasn't quite like that, Jack. My mom and dad never agreed with your parents for keeping it from you, but it wasn't their decision to make. Who knows what it's like to watch your baby get grabbed from your arms? They thought they were doing the right thing," Andy said, raising his eyebrows.

Jack sighed. Andy was right. "I suppose I can understand the secrecy for all these years, but the whole mission to get the Vitax, what was the point?"

Andy stood and paced with his arms behind his back. "Everyone who is part of S.O.U.P. is special. There's something in all of us that gives us unique abilities and senses. You have grown up as a normal boy, Jack, you needed to be tested for that special thing, just to make sure it hadn't left you since birth. Every one of us has had to take a similar test. Some don't pass the first time."

"Did I?"

Andy dashed to the bedside again. "Did you? With flying colors! You deciphered codes and messages quicker than some life forms who've been training in the academy for decades. Laughing at you—no way, most of us are in awe. You know that room with the Vitax and those booby traps? I invented all of that."

"I thought it was all a bit *Indiana Jones*."

"Yeah, my favorite! You know me! You worked all that out because you're special."

Jack shook his head. "I dunno, Andy, I don't feel special. I mean, I'm pretty good with a soccer ball but how can that help pacify an entire galaxy or keep me safe from being abducted?"

"That's where your life is going to change for the better, Jack. No more Woodland Main School for me and you. As of next week, intensive training begins for you to learn all that S.O.U.P. does and exactly what's out there in our galaxy. Forget everything that you've read or watched about outer space. N.A.S.A. only knows what S.O.U.P. wants them to know. We're the only ones who know the real truth, trust me."

"I want to, I do but I..." Jack still couldn't convince himself this was right.

Andy sat back down on the edge of the bed. "Has your life given you everything you've ever wanted so far?" He held out his hand to stop Jack from answering. "I can answer that—no, it hasn't. You've found your life utterly boring, and you are fed up with being so ordinary, right? That's because it's in you. You've always been destined for more. Well, now your chance has come to be the new Jack

Mills, S.O.U.P. agent extraordinaire."

Jack shook his head. Andy used the most bizarre words. Just then, the door opened and in strode Roxy.

"Hiya," she said, plonking herself down on the bed. "Are you ready for the adventure of a lifetime?"

Jack smiled. Being an alien clearly made no difference to Roxy; she was simply Roxy, whatever her species.

"Am I?" he asked her back.

"I'll say! You were a pleasure to go on a mission with, even if it was a fake one! Don't underestimate yourself, Jack, you solved some seriously hard puzzles, you're more ready for this than you think."

Jack thought for a moment. "There are some answers I still need."

"Go on," Roxy said, rolling to her front and putting her chin in her hands.

"I suppose all that stuff you told me about your dad leaving you was made up."

"Sadly not."

"But you're an alien," Jack said.

"So what? You think humans are the only species allowed to have family problems? I wish it wasn't true, you know."

"Oh, I'm sorry. I guess I didn't expect aliens to have families," Jack said, scratching his head. He clearly had a lot to learn.

"Well, we do," Roxy said, smiling. "What else do you want to know?"

Jack thought. "That stinky brown stuff, was it really alien poo?"

"No, it's fuel for the spaceships, a substance we bring over from a planet in The Ring Galaxy." Roxy laughed.

"The moving car in number 2's drive?"

"Alien. And the one at number 3."

"What, like real Transformers?" Jack turned to Andy, his eyes opening wider.

"In a way," Andy said.

"And that shadow thing from the passageways, what was that?"

"A Drohen," Roxy said.

"What's a Drohen?"

"Kind of like a security guard," Andy said.

"Yeah, a security guard made of emptiness straight from the deep, dark planet of Halja!" Roxy boomed, deepening her voice.

"Halja?"

"Hell!"

Jack looked at Roxy. Joke, or no joke? It was impossible to tell. He wasn't sure how to respond so decided to move on. "Your hair? Is it real?"

"One hundred percent wig! Look." Roxy whipped off her curly, white hair.

Jack grimaced at her lumpy, bald head. "No, I prefer you with the wig."

"Me too! Can you do something for me?" Roxy asked, popping her hair back on and adjusting it into position.

"Maybe," Jack answered.

"Will you teach me to play soccer? It looks awesome."

"It's overrated, Roxy, I'll never understand the fascination with that sport," Andy said, dismissing her question with a wave of his hand.

"Well, I want to learn, okay?"

"I wouldn't bother. There are heaps of better things to learn about."

"I didn't ask you."

"You should have."

"Should I?"

"Yes."

"Why?"

As Andy and Roxy bickered, Jack leaned back into the pillow. From now on, things were going to be tough. Aliens were going to come for him. And soon. But part of him wasn't worried. Part of him buzzed with excitement. With happiness. Looking from Andy to Roxy and back again, he thought of what Andy said. Jack really did feel like he belonged there, with them. It was strange. The past week had been scary, terrifying even, but not once could he remember feeling bored. Galaxy saving had actually been a lot of fun. And to be a part of S.O.U.P. To hang with Dad. Invent things together. Jack couldn't fight the smile.

So this was it, his future. Whether he liked it or not. Were things really so bad? New doors were about to open—and having already visited the underground world he knew there were plenty to choose from. Perhaps his dream would come true, and he could have a ride in that awesome gold spaceship and learn how to read the alien writing.

"By the way." Andy looked at Jack, disturbing his thoughts. "What's this I hear about you wearing luminous green boxers with puppies?"

Jack and Roxy glanced at one another. After a second, they both erupted into uncontrollable laughter.

TO BE CONTINUED...

Acknowledgments

I have so many people to thank but must start with my parents. You guys are my rocks. I would never have pursued this dream without you and your support. Thank you, eternally.

Thanks to Jack, Toby, and Harry. You three provide all the inspiration I ever need to write. And thank you, Dan; it's a real honor to know you enjoyed the book when it isn't something you'd ever dream of picking up and reading.

To Sandra Glover for offering insightful, spot-on critiques that took this story from average to incredible. To Rebecca Carpenter for your dazzling editing skills, and to E.L.Wicker for so much, but in particular the orange juice!

To Paul Mudie for your patience with me and for creating a stunning cover.

Thanks to the many wonderful people who have provided feedback, left reviews, and are a part of my writing community I love so dearly.

And thank you to all the readers who have picked up *Winell Road* and are now part of Jack's journey. Oh boy, it's about to get crazy!

About the Author

Kate is an Englishwoman living on the Gold Coast in Australia with her family. She writes, reads, edits, and dreams, but not always in that order.

If you have enjoyed *Winell Road* and would like to find out more about Kate and what's to come for Jack and the rest of S.O.U.P., sign up for Kate's newsletter via her website.

www.katefosterauthor.com

And finally, there is no better way to hug an author than to leave a book review or send them a message. Kate is always keen to engage with her readers, so feel free to get in touch.

CPSIA information can be obtained
at www.ICGtesting.com
Printed in the USA
FSHW020319050419
56931FS